ASYLUM

Sherry Logsden

"The Power of Pen
and Paper"

ASYLUM

A NOVEL

SHERRY
LOGSDON

 WinePressPublishing
Great Books, Defined.

WinePress Publishing is honored to present this title in partnership with the author. The views expressed or implied in this work are those of the author. WinePress provides our imprint seal representing design excellence, creative content and high quality production. To learn more about Responsible Publishing™ visit www.winepresspublishing.com.

ISBN 13: 978-1-4141-2318-9
ISBN 10: 1-4141-2318-3
Library of Congress Catalog Card Number: 2012904171

"How can a doctor judge a woman's sanity by merely bidding her good morning and refusing to hear her pleas for release? Even the sick ones know it is useless to say anything, for the answer will be that it is their imagination" (Nellie Bly, Journalist and Author of *Ten Days in a Mad-House,* 1887).

The House

Standing high upon the hill
Its features cold and gray
A house that held inside its walls
A child who could not play

She could not play for she was but
A prisoner in a cell
Who had to do what she was told
But never could she tell

Not only could she never tell
But never could she see
The way that other children played
The way that it should be

To play as if a beauty queen
With powder and a purse
Or mending scratches on a doll
Just like a real life nurse

Her world was but a darkened room
Madness filled the air
To see it for the way it was
Her mind would never dare

So now she's gotten far away
But peace she'll never find
For terrors hidden in the house
Now hide inside her mind

CONTENTS

ACKNOWLEDGMENTS

I would like to thank everyone who helped this book become a reality—Becki, and Rosemary, for spending so much time reading and editing, Bonnie and Mom for reading and liking the story. If just one of you had discouraged me, I might have stopped writing.

I would like to thank my husband for having the patience that I did not have many times, and my children, Amy, Kyle, and Ryan Jaggers for never complaining because they grew up with a mother lost in her own world. For their support, I am most grateful.

AUTHOR'S NOTE

I began writing this book almost twenty years ago. The length of time became intentional. It took me this long to let it go. The process has been an outlet for me. I delved into a fictional world and began living through the characters. I took misplaced worries and fears and transferred them to written pages. This book has provided therapy throughout many battles of my life.

Although written as fiction, this novel is based on many candid and factual happenings. As this story reveals, the injustices done to women throughout history are great in magnitude.

There are characters in *Asylum* who discover the healing power of journaling and writing poetry. The pen and the paper are by far mightier than the sword; this has certainly been true for me.

PART ONE

THE JOURNEY, 1896

CHAPTER 1

I boarded the *S.S. Farnassia* with the hopes of a bright and beautiful future.

It was but a false hope, for I found the atmosphere on the ship to be no different than the one that had characterized my sixteen years in Scotland. Both were dark and disturbing. Other than *awful*, I had never found a word to describe my life. Once on board, I found awful to be a term most useful in describing steerage, the bottom of the bottom.

The conditions on the ship were insufferable, the sleeping compartments no more than five feet high with two tiers of cots so narrow they hardly provided enough room to turn over. People were packed closely together. The smell was dreadful, and the air and light inadequate, making the filth seem even worse.

By the second day, I already missed the sight of land and the feel of clean, fresh air on my face. I longed for the tranquility of watching clouds roll across an open sky. As a child, I had often imagined the clouds to be creatures put high above the earth to protect and watch over me. When I had done something bad they would turn dark and angry and scold me with their rumbles. In school, I frequently made up stories and played childish games. My teacher, who concluded that I acted in such ways because I lacked a mother, reprimanded me repeatedly. The truth was that I was just trying to relieve the boredom and dreariness of my life.

As I started undressing for bed, I could feel the eyes of other passengers watching my movements, reminding me once again that I was not home, alone in my bedroom. I pulled my sleeping gown over my head then pulled my dress off from underneath—a feat I had adapted to in a mere two nights' time.

I hurriedly leaped onto the narrow cot as if something or someone might suddenly jump out from under it. I had gotten into bed like that for as long as I could remember. I knew it would be a while before I would fall asleep. In fact, sometimes I did not sleep at all. Instead, I just tossed and turned, listening to the strange sounds of the night, watching shadows float across the walls. Many nights I simply jiggled my foot, a habit I had developed to keep myself awake. It was not a case of insomnia with me but a case of fear. Within the darkness came a rage that filled the air and consumed my very soul, a weakness that even the most cowardly would be ashamed of.

As daylight approached and the darkness gave way to a pale shade of gray, I opened my eyes and again forgot for an instant where I was. Looking around at the forlorn souls around me, and seeing so much suffering, I could hardly feel pity for myself.

I would need to play many games in my mind to endure this harsh and frightful journey to America.

CHAPTER 2

As I awoke, I looked over at a restless, what I guessed to be middle-aged woman. She had an intense, troubled look about her, even as she sent a smile my way. Miriam had introduced herself to me as we were boarding the ship on that first day. We had said little to each other since then. I had chosen the cot next to hers. A familiar face in a seemingly harsh crowd brought comfort.

I was sure she wondered why a young girl would travel without a companion, just as I questioned a woman of her age traveling alone. I pictured possible scenarios, but dismissed them all. This was another kind of game I played with myself. I took a situation and made up guesses as to what the truth behind it might be. My minimal experiences in travel and life meant my guesses were also limited, placing them nowhere near the truth most of the time.

I questioned everything about the ship, the passengers, and the conditions we were forced to travel in. Looking at Miriam now, I wondered if she might be able to supply at least some of the answers I so desperately longed for.

"Miriam. Why are we confined to the bottom of such a large ship?" I asked, a little surprised at my boldness.

"Only the people in first class are worth the time to be shown the sight of the moon and stars at night and the warmth of the sun during the day," Miriam answered.

"Why does being first class make one worth more than those in steerage? Are we not worth the time it would take to allow us on deck, if only for a few minutes a day?"

"Being first class does not make one actually worth more. 'First class' just means one has more money. Although, I guess, in some ways that does make one worth more." Miriam let out a giggly laugh that sounded quite childlike for a woman her age. "It is just the way of the world, child, not God's way. That is all I know."

I lay and pondered how money could make one person worth more than another, or why one person could be loved more than another. If all people are pulled from their mothers' wombs naked at birth, then are not all people essentially the same? If a person is lucky enough to have more money than someone else or parents who love her more than someone else's parents love their child, do those circumstances make the person worth more? It seemed to me that it should only make that person luckier. But then again, luck was something I knew little of.

I wanted to ask Miriam other questions, but before I had formed them in my mind, I began to feel quite ill. The nausea overtook me as I expelled what little contents my stomach held. Though I had eaten no more than a few bites since boarding the ship, my raw throat and the miserable nausea did not relent.

"It will get better. It is only seasickness. It too will pass," Miriam reassured me.

Miriam's smile consisted of two missing front teeth. She reminded me of a picture I had seen once of my own grandmother, only without the missing teeth. There was a sparkle in Miriam's eyes that hardships and regrets had not taken from her.

If only I could expel the guilt within me as easily as I had the food. I did not know if the guilt dwelled within my heart or within my mind. Did I think about it because I felt it, or did I feel it because I thought about it? The question seemed to constantly spiral in my mind without ever settling on an answer. I only knew that the guilt thrived. The guilt had become who I was and what I believed I was: a child well acquainted with guilt and grief.

CHAPTER 3

By the next morning, with stomach eased and the cobwebs cleared from my mind, I felt that I might actually live. I turned to Miriam and could see that she too was awake.

My curiosity had finally gotten the better of me.

"Miriam, would it be too forward of me to ask why you travel alone?" Although I wanted to know her story, I prayed she would not ask me the same.

"No child, it would not be forward of you at all, merely friendly. I would take it to mean you care."

Miriam shared her reason with a kind of sadness. "I chose to travel alone. My son wished to come to Germany and accompany me to America. I would not hear of it. He also wished to pay my fare but I would hear nothing of that, either. I wanted to carry my own weight into the New World, and that is what I will be doing.

"Honestly, it has been my own fear that has kept me in Germany for so long. I would not be a burden to my son. He and his wife are expecting a baby soon. I am to be a grandmother. My son wants his child to know its grandmother, and they have plenty of room in their home. He is a lawyer and makes good wages. He says I could be a great help to them; which is pure rubbish. He is just making excuses to give his mother a reason to make such a journey. I do love my boy, but I fear a burden is what I will be, nonetheless."

"I agree with your son, Miriam. Family should ensure the well-being of their members, and I see where you could be of great help to your son and his wife, as well as bring them much happiness." I spoke as if I knew all about families, when, in truth, all I really knew about was the lack of one. My limited knowledge came by watching and listening to others.

"Burden or not, child, if I had known how bad steerage really was, I would have thought twice before turning down my son's offer to pay for my ticket. An old woman's silly pride."

I did not think Miriam nearly as old as she professed to be, and I was sure Miriam's son would have been quite upset to know that she was traveling in steerage. How funny the mind works, I thought. I was consumed by guilt for having survived my mother in childbirth and Miriam was consumed by the fear of burdening her son. I wondered, did all people carry such weights on their backs?

Miriam stared into space as she continued talking. "My son, Paul, was a good boy who never brought any trouble to his mother. Life was not easy for a boy with no father. I have seen the marks on his skin, inflicted by the other boys in school; I knew of the cruel taunting he endured. Life was becoming harder for Jews in Germany," Miriam said wearily. "I knew I had to get my Paul to America to live with my brother, but I did not have enough money for us both. Anti-Semitism was growing stronger by the day. My heart ached the day of his departure. I'll never forget the pain in his voice as he asked me why he had to leave me and if I had stopped loving him.

"'It is because I love you that you must go,' I told him. I tried to explain that his Papa did not die for him to die as well.

He left enough money to send Paul to America to get a good education. At fifteen, Paul was a promising student and I knew America would offer him the best opportunity to further his studies. Life would be better for him there. I told him to go and make his Papa and me proud. Paul's uncle is a good man and I knew he would treat my son like his own. He had sent a letter saying he would sponsor Paul in America. I told Paul to keep that letter close and not to lose it. I promised him that I would follow soon. Then I swallowed my own pain, hugged him, and sent him to America." Miriam bowed her head and cried as she relived the scene in her mind.

"Time goes by so fast," Miriam said. "The years went by like seconds on a clock. His uncle kept me up on his progress. Paul took up so well in America. He made good grades and worked hard. I feared that somehow my presence would interfere with that. That was fifteen years ago."

I watched as Miriam's face softened and her eyes became glazed. It looked as if Miriam believed that by staring hard and long enough she could make whatever she was thinking come true. I thought to myself that it would surely break her spirit if this venture did not turn out well.

"Have you had breakfast?" I asked, trying to lighten the mood and change the subject before Miriam asked for my story.

"Is that what you would call it, *breakfast*?" Miriam answered with a lilt in her voice.

We both laughed and I decided this trip might not be so awful after all.

"And how was your sleep?" Miriam asked.

Her question caught me off guard. I hesitated and then reached up and felt a tear in the corner of my eye. No one had ever asked me about my sleep. How silly to tear up at such a thing! Her comfort was something I needed, I realized.

"I slept as well as one could in such dreadful conditions," I answered. But as I rose from the cot, I once again felt sick. Was this wretched seasickness never going to cease? I prayed that it would end soon.

CHAPTER 4

As I lay still and talked with Miriam, I noticed a young woman standing just beyond our cots. She seemed to be straining to hear our conversation. Why take note of us? Why was she in steerage at all, for that matter? She looked out of place. She looked worth more.

Her eyes were large and expressive and turned from a sparkling emerald green to a dark and serious jade when they met mine. She had a high, impressive forehead, giving her a very different look from the Scottish girls I had grown up with. Her nose was long, straight, and prominent; her ears small and close to her head. She had pulled her tawny blonde hair tightly beneath a large, decorative hat. Over her well-proportioned frame, she wore a slim-fitting dress made of a pressed gray fabric, buttoned high beneath her chin. I expected to see such a dress on someone much older.

"May I join your conversation?" the woman asked in German.

Miriam translated her words into English for me.

The woman repeated her question in English.

"There is not much of a conversation to join," replied Miriam. "Besides, I've got to stand up and get my aching body moving. If I sit much longer, it will take both of you to get me off this tiny bed that only one good hip fits on." She rolled out of the cot and bounced off the floor like a child's rubber ball.

The young woman and I laughed until our sides ached. I could not remember ever laughing so hard. It felt good and helped me to forget the tossing of the ship.

The young woman extended her hand, "My name is Norna Strom. It is nice to meet you."

I was not quite sure why Norna Strom thought it nice to meet me, other than the laugh we had shared, and I felt that credit did not belong to me.

"Isobel McFadden," I said with a hesitancy I felt sure Norna could sense.

With the introductions behind us, Norna and I began to chat. The words came as easily as if we had known each other for years instead of minutes.

I had been correct in assuming Norna belonged in first class.

"Isobel, do you mind if I spend my time with you here in steerage? I find the people in first class overly stuffy and boring," requested Norna at the conclusion of our conversation.

"Of course I do not mind. If you are sure that is what you want," I answered, feeling glad to have made the acquaintance of someone so interesting.

I could not imagine being in steerage by choice, but was too happy for the company to question her motives. Norna spoke with such vitality and strength that her voice put me at ease almost immediately; a rare thing.

I had learned to be cautious of what sprang from peoples' mouths after encountering many who spat out words that amounted to nothing more than lies. I did not feel this from Norna, but still could not let down my guard. I hoped that someday this barrier of caution would subside.

I had found comfort from Miriam and friendship from Norna. I began to allow myself to believe the journey would prove more tolerable than I had first imagined.

CHAPTER 5

I soon learned that Norna and I were surprisingly close in age. When she entered the room, everyone's eyes followed her. From the way she dressed and carried herself, I had believed her to be some years older. Her laughter and amusing stories commanded attention. She always had a new tale to tell, and constantly talked of going to America to live with her older brother. He was only five years older than she, making him twenty-three, and a full-fledged doctor.

She did not, however, mention her parents, and I dared not ask for fear she would ask about mine.

"So, do you look anything like this brother of yours of whom you speak so fondly?" I asked.

"People say I do," Norna said. "We both have blonde hair, but his has beautiful golden streaks where mine is dark and drab. Though our commonalities are frequently pointed out I always felt that he is the better looking by far. Philip would dare to disagree, telling me that I was far too critical of myself and unquestionably too serious. Of course, Philip has persistently been biased and takes nothing too seriously. I have always envied and adored my brother's carefree and courageous attitude, but I have never been able to follow his lead."

As I listened to Norna talk about her brother, I felt the warmth of her pride in him, and envied the love they shared. I had no brothers or sisters of my own and often wondered what it would be like to love someone that much. I had neither given nor received that kind of love. That sad fact left me empty inside.

I understood what Norna meant about thinking so miserably of herself. Many times I had cursed my own skinny body and wretched hair, which willfully sprang out of my head in every possible direction. Unfortunately, it was also the brightest shade of red. With age, my hatred of my appearance had lessened. My skinny frame had kept many the drunkards away, convincing them that I was younger than my actual age—a blessing in disguise. And there was something about my hair, hanging wildly and falling loosely to my waist that made me feel free, like I belonged to myself and no one could make me into something I was not. I refused to pull it up. That little bit of rebellion had taken me a long way in masking my emotions.

CHAPTER 6

W hat is it you are going to do while living with your brother?" I asked Norna one morning as we sat chatting.

"My main duty will be to keep house and cook. At least that is what my brother thinks. You know we Germans are supposedly known for our neatness. He thinks that will occupy my time and keep me out of trouble. Cleaning will not be all I do. I want to write. My dream is to be a journalist, and work for a newspaper and have my own column every week."

When she talked about writing, Norna's face brightened with such conviction and determination that I felt certain she could do it. Her eyes were driving and dominant, her voice filled with willpower. Norna would never know the meaning of failure. Of that I was certain.

"What will you write about?" I had never known a real writer before, though I had secretly written poems as long as I could remember. What else could one enjoy writing?

"I want to write about all the awful things that are happening in the world. I will not cover them up with sweetness and hope, when there is none." Norna paused. "I am down here not only because I enjoy your company in steerage but also to watch the people. There are no stories in first class, only gossip and talk of all the things their money will buy when they get to America. Steerage is where the real stories are. This is where people struggle just to make it day by day. The sacrifices and the injustices of the world are right here."

"I would never have guessed you would want to write about such things," I blurted. "I expected you would think more about recipes and how to sew and mend, about fashion and women's things." The words were out of my mouth before I could blink. I immediately wished I could take them back. How stupid of me to say such a thing.

"Do not look so horrified. You said what most people think and dare never say. That infuriates me, and it is exactly why I want to write the truth. My whole way of thinking changed when I read a book I found in my aunt's library. I knew then that I wanted to be a writer. Have you ever heard of Mary Wollstonecraft?"

I repeated the name but was sure I had never heard it pronounced before. I hoped it was not someone I was supposed to have learned about in school. I did not want Norna to know that soon after my eleventh birthday my father removed me from school and put me to work alongside him in a pub. Though I had missed out on many school lessons, I had learned many lessons of life.

"Well I am sure, Isobel, you have not if you have to think so hard. She is someone you would never forget. Have you ever heard of the book *Frankenstein*?"

Now, *that* I had heard of. My teacher had talked about the book and the creature in school. He had discussed that specific book because the author had spent some time in Scotland. Mr. Graham took great pride in his Scottish birthright and felt greatly touched by anyone who hailed from our homeland. Sir Arthur Conan Doyle and Robert Louis Stevenson were by far his favorite authors. Robert Louis Stevenson had also written a book about a kind of monster, called *The Strange Case of Dr. Jekyll and Mr. Hyde.* "I am aware of that book." I answered.

"It was written by Mary Shelley. Mary Wollstonecraft is her mother." Norna said it as if this piece of missing information would clear up everything. I must have looked even more daft than usual.

"Mary Wollstonecraft is my inspiration as a writer. In 1792, when she was just thirty-three years old, she wrote *A Vindication of the Rights of Woman.* It was wonderfully written, although many disagree. Mary argued in her writings that women were first of all human beings, and therefore entitled by God's creation to the same benefits and equalities as men. She was a fiery feminist. She was also not afraid to be an English Jacobin; she supported the French Revolution."

I listened intently as Norna went on. "Many people argued that she could never be a fit role-model for a young woman, swearing she was unstable, that she suffered from nervous illnesses, and some even suggested that she attempted suicide. I find her the most thrilling and rebellious woman who ever picked up pen and paper. She had a spirit ahead of her time. Mary's body and my own may have been born years apart, but our souls were born as one. She was, and forever will be, nothing less than an inspirational genius.

"Mary Wollstonecraft said, 'Strengthen the female mind by enlarging it, and there will be an end to blind obedience.' I could forever quote her words as if they were as my own," Norna said as she crossed her hands over her heart.

I had never heard anyone speak with such conviction in my life. The passion in her voice gave me goose bumps. Not even the clerics who stood outside the pub preaching of sin and damnation for all who entered sounded that adamant. How I wanted to be like Norna, so full of fire and fury, not afraid to show emotions. I longed for the courage to take a stand for what I believed with no care for what others thought.

CHAPTER 7

After listening to Norna, I too thought that Mary Wollstonecraft sounded like a wonderful writer. I might never have had the courage to say it, but I admired anyone who said women should not be expected to do everything men told them.

"I like the sound of this woman writer. Whatever became of her?" I asked.

"Such a shame, at the age of thirty-eight she died from complications of giving birth to her second daughter, Mary Shelley."

I shivered as soon as the words of death and childbirth left Norna's lips. Had she noticed?

Norna went on, "Other than my aunt I have never told anyone about my secret desire to write whatever pours out of my heart, even if it is against what the whole world believes. I do not want to hear anyone say what a woman cannot do. I want to put my words on paper and make them come alive so people feel those words. There is so much horror and despair in the world, so much to fear, and people simply cover it up with their money and prestige." Norna spoke with tears in her eyes and a face filled with sadness.

I wanted to tell Norna that I felt a terrible kind of trepidation too. My feelings of guilt were even worse than my fear. I had never talked to anyone about these and I wanted to ask Norna if she too felt guilt, but I was ashamed. What if she said she did not? I had found something that bound us together, and could not risk losing it. It gave me a kind of strength to talk so openly about fear. Maybe in time I could ask her about other feelings such as shame and regret.

"But that is enough about me and my Mary Wollstonecraft," she said. "Why are you going to America?"

I wondered only for a second whether I should tell her the truth. There was something inside me that had come to trust this girl. Maybe I was being naïve, or maybe I just needed to talk. Either way, I risked sharing a portion of the truth.

"I am going to be employed by Dr. William Helsley. My father and he were in contact with one another. I am not quite sure what I will be doing. My father answered a newspaper advertisement that Dr. Helsley placed in the Edinburgh newspaper, and Dr. Helsley wrote my father that I sounded perfect for the job."

Norna looked at me quizzically. "I am totally perplexed as to why someone would go to America without a clue as to the exact purpose. I am sure you have your reason, but I am also sure it cannot be good. I suppose my situation is not all that good, either. I will be nineteen next month and have been lost to the world far too long. I can hardly believe I have been living with my aunt for nearly five years. Time has stood still, yet hastily sped by at the same time. Thank God for Aunt Iris. If not for her I would surely have been locked away in some hospital being spoon fed to this day."

For some reason my instincts told me I did not want to ask Norna what she meant. Instead, I squealed in hopes of changing the subject.

"Look, there they go again!" The rats consistently scurried across the floor. In reality they did not really trouble me so much. I had seen plenty scurrying across the floors of the pub where my father and I worked and where we lived upstairs.

I started feeling sick again, not sure if it was seasickness or the stench around me making my stomach turn. The food was sparse and beginning to rot, and its rank odor permeated the air. How I wished for scones and apple butter. I had had very little to drink. The water we drank was warm and smelled foul with a greasy film on top, whereas the water in the washroom was cold salt water.

If sacrifices and injustices were what Norna wanted, then she had found them in steerage. I doubted if Norna had ever eaten anything as miserable as stale bread and lukewarm soup, but she ate it with no complaints. I had no doubt that, with her stamina, Norna could handle whatever faced her in life.

CHAPTER 8

The list of ill steerage passengers seemed to multiply daily. Over the course of two weeks on the ship, three children and a mother had died. I wondered at the life that would have awaited them in America, a life they would never live. Hopelessness overtook me. Would the misery of life in steerage ever end? Norna leaned over and whispered into my ear, "Just remember, it will be over soon, and you will be in America."

I had never met anyone with such a high degree of sensitivity. It seemed she could even read my thoughts.

I tried Norna's way of thinking. I spent more time listening to the stories of the splendid opportunities awaiting us in America and less time dwelling on the horrors of possible deportation at Ellis Island. I tried to close my ears to the stories of what would happen to those who did not pass the medical tests and would be shuttled onto another ship to return home. I would surely die if that happened to me.

I knew sixteen was not very old, but I had begun to feel quite aged and alone. I was going to miss my newly acquired friends when the time of our arrival came.

"Norna, there is something I have been meaning to ask you. What does anti-Semitism mean? I have heard the word a few times before. Miriam used it when she talked about her son."

"It is a kind of hatred manifested toward Jews." She wrinkled her brow in an expression of deep thought. "The Jews have been accused of not respecting humanity. In my opinion and that of many others, anti-Semitism is inhumane and provokes some of the most intolerable acts conducted by mankind, because one group of people dares to judge another. People say Jews are unclean, leprous people. It all makes me sick," Norna said, as she slammed her fist into her lap.

"How could you possibly know so much about everything?" I asked.

"By reading, I told you there is nothing like the power of pen and paper. That words envelope the knowledge of the world. Do not ever forget that."

Wherever I ended up in America, I hoped there would be a bountiful number of books so I could fill my head as full of information as Norna's.

Just when I feared the sea was to be my permanent home, we heard someone bellow that land had been sighted. Norna and I had spoken daily of our yearning to see the shoreline of America. We longed to see the great Statue of Liberty that represented freedom for all people, even those who were *worth* less.

Now that the day we dreamed of had arrived, it suddenly filled me with dread. I had convinced myself that it could not be as bad as I imagined, but I had learned that when one does not think things can get any worse, they usually do.

I wondered if Norna was feeling any of this same nervousness, but I presumed that was silly. Norna was going to live with her brother and not some stranger whom she knew nothing about.

It was during our last visit before leaving the ship that Norna stepped beside me and reached for my hand. "I will miss you, Isobel. The girl with more hair than body has nurtured the fight in me that I have been looking so hard to find."

I could not imagine Norna ever losing a fight or that I could nurture anything.

"Isobel, take this. It is my brother's address in New York City. If you need me, this is where you will find me."

With a tearful nod, Norna thrust the paper into my hand. The look in her eyes frightened me.

If I had known what lay ahead, I would have indisputably believed Norna a mind reader. Instead, I thanked her for being so kind.

CHAPTER 9

As I stepped onto dry land, I felt more excited than exhausted and afraid, almost forgetting the dreaded inspection process ahead. Those of us who had spent the voyage in steerage were being ferried to Ellis Island, where we would undergo both legal and medical inspections.

I watched carefully as a somber woman towering at least two feet above me pinned a name tag bearing several numbers to the front of my dress. I was fingerprinted and poked with needles. As a distraction, I began to read the expressions on all the faces of those surrounding me. Some were so overwhelmed, I was not sure they were strong enough to undergo the tests, let alone pass them.

On completion of the first examinations, we were immediately directed to wait in yet another line where announcements were made about what we were to expect next. These announcements were repeated multiple times in many other languages. If all went well, the entire process was expected to take no longer than five hours. With just this small amount of information, relief replaced fear.

A woman in a white uniform began searching through the unruliness of my hair, checking for nits. Next a doctor checked my eyes to determine if I had glaucoma or trachoma, and then I was taken to another doctor who checked for signs of other illnesses. In my confusion, I could not remember all the examinations that I had to undergo.

I looked around, fearing for so many, when from the corner of my eye, I noticed a young woman consoling two small children clinging to her skirt. Their bare feet were smudged with grime, and both were crying most hysterically. My pulse began to beat rapidly. What right did I have to complain when there where so many worse off than me? I wanted to be generous and help the young mother, yet I knew I had to help myself at the moment, and so I could only hope they would be well.

How I longed for the strength and good sense to fulfill my purpose in America.

CHAPTER 10

As I waited, I heard soft weeping, and knew it was someone who had failed the barrage of tests. Nervously, I sat and waited my turn. There would be no soft tears for me. They would have to send me kicking and wailing. I would not go back without a fight and was already planning what I would do if they told me I had failed. Just as my imagination began to unfold, I was handed a card. This was it. I nervously turned the card around so I could read my future. I had passed the tests. I felt but a brief moment of glory and satisfaction before my sorrow for those who had not passed began to set in.

I had not seen Norna since leaving the ship, and already missed her strong words and fanciful imagination. While standing in line, I had heard that first class passengers did not have to undergo all the examinations. They were quickly checked out on the ship. It was true that money does buy privileges. But having to stand in line would have been no hindrance to Norna; it would only have given her more things to write about.

As I sat patiently on a wooden bench, not sure what I was to do next, I noticed a youthful woman in a dark suit and shirtwaist blouse waving a handkerchief at a young man. How my heart started to flutter thinking it to be Norna. However, as the woman moved closer, I saw that it was not. Without Norna, I feared my strength would begin to fail.

I looked around thinking I had heard someone calling my name. Upon hearing it once again, I turned and saw none other than Miriam. She stood with a man who had to be her son. They both shared the same twinkle in their eyes.

Miriam squeezed me tightly. It was good to feel her arms embrace me.

"Isobel, you must meet my Paul. Is he not the most handsome man you have ever seen?"

He stood over a foot taller than Miriam, quite sturdy-looking, with thick and curly hair the color of cinnamon. His broad, beaming smile was filled with warmth and sincerity.

"He is, to be sure," I laughed.

Paul embraced me with the warmth of an old friend.

"It is so good to meet a friend of my mother's. I must thank you for keeping her company on the ship. I am sure it was a rough journey, especially since my mother has been so pig-headed about the whole thing," he joked, while grinning at his mother.

"I am a grandmother," Miriam exclaimed. "She was born yesterday. We are on our way to the hospital. They named her Paulie, Paulie Cohen, after my Paul. You must come and visit. You must see my new grandchild." Miriam looked so happy and relieved she no longer carried the look of sickness.

"Are you going to be all right here alone, Isobel?" Paul asked. "Do you have a ride?"

"I am fine. Thank you for asking. I have someone meeting me. Do give your wife and baby a hug for me."

Miriam embraced me once again as she spoke, "I will miss you and I hope you will find as much happiness in America as

I already have. I was such a fool to worry so much and wait so long."

"Indeed you were," I said as I returned Miriam's hug. "Indeed you were."

CHAPTER 11

M iriam and I bid our goodbyes and waved to one another. I now felt two holes in my heart, one for Norna and another for Miriam.

I returned to my bench. As soon as I began to wonder how Dr. Helsley would ever locate me, I realized I no longer cared. If I could leave without my sponsor, I would walk the streets and find my own work. I was strong and very capable of fending for myself.

I was tired of feeling weak and becoming increasingly weary of the whole ordeal. In truth, I did not trust my father. What work had he found me? I replayed our last conversation, searching again for clues to my future.

"Isobel, it is time for you to be on your way and fend for yourself," my father announced while wiping down the bar as I scrubbed the floors. *"I intend for you to make your own way in the world. I have kept you sheltered long enough."*

I wanted to laugh, but dared not. The wrath of Michael McFadden was fierce, and one I did not wish to bring upon myself. But the thought of having been sheltered was indeed laughable. I had never been sheltered a day in my life. I had worked for everything

I ever received. If not for the grace of my grandmother helping out those first few years, I am sure I would not have survived at all.

"You will be boarding a ship tomorrow for America."

"Tomorrow?" I froze at the suddenness of it all, but quickly realized I would be the glad for it.

"Will be a good thing, indeed." I would not let him see how his words had unnerved me. I had never even visited another town before, much less another country. "I will gladly go."

"It is time to do away with the demons of the past," he muttered under his breath.

My father was the only demon I cared to do away with.

How could he blame me for killing my mother? Did he not think how much better my life would have been if she had lived? What else did he blame me for? There had to be more, but what? I could not imagine what else I had done that had turned his hatred toward me with such a vengeance.

I grew more nervous by the moment. Just as I made my decision to wait no longer for Dr. Helsley and to take off on my own, I heard a gentleman behind me clearing his throat.

"Miss McFadden, is that you?" he asked.

I turned to answer yes but could only stare. He was a squatty man, as round as he was tall, with a brutishness about his face. His eyebrows were heavy and close-knit set over nervous eyes and a large moustache covered most of his mouth. He kept checking his pocket watch as if he were late for an important engagement. I could find nothing appealing about this man. Never would I have chosen to work for him.

"Dr. Helsley?"

He confirmed that he was indeed Dr. Helsley and that I was late. I did not know that I was expected at any certain time.

"I thought your father said that you were sixteen." His face revealed his displeasure. "You do not look a day over fourteen. Such unruly hair, and do you not ever eat? You are even skinnier and more unusual looking than your father described."

Rage boiled within me, not only over his rude comments, but the heartless laughter that came with them. Why had he and my father discussed my appearance? What did that have to do with my working? I felt as if Dr. Helsley and my father had been making a deal over a goat or a pig, not a human.

Before I could speak for myself, Dr. Helsley continued, "We will be spending the night at the Waldorf Hotel. You will find it most suitable, I am sure. We must be on our way."

CHAPTER 12

S uitable" was hardly the word I would have chosen. As we descended the cable car I could hardly believe my eyes. On the corner of Fifth Avenue and Thirty-Third Street stood the most magnificent building I had ever seen. I now knew one thing about Dr. Helsley: he was a very wealthy man. I never dreamed of entering such a magnificent building, let alone spending the night in one.

"Stop wasting time gaping, Miss McFadden, and do hurry. We are to rise early to board a train."

Dr. Helsley finalized arrangements for our night's stay and I was escorted to my room by a rather lean, lanky young man. He had a slender face covered entirely with freckles. Once he opened his mouth, it never closed again. His constant chatter rolled straight through my head without ever stopping to make contact with my thoughts. I did not understand a thing he was talking about. I simply smiled and nodded.

"I take it this is your first time at the Waldorf?"

"Aye," I answered, as dumbfounded as I felt.

"Oh, so you are not from America? Let me guess, Ireland?"

"No, I am from Scotland."

"Same thing, you people are everywhere."

"What people are everywhere?" I asked.

"Immigrants, but I don't mean anything bad about it. I like it."

As I began to correct the young man that Ireland and Scotland were most definitely not the same thing, he opened the door to the loveliest room I had ever seen. All I could do was stand with my mouth agape.

The young man began to laugh, "Well, wherever you're from Miss, I see the room meets with your approval. It's nice to see someone else who appreciates grandness and beauty as much as I do. It is marvelous, isn't it? The Waldorf has thirteen stories with four hundred and fifty rooms. I want to own a hotel just like this one day, and I will."

I had met a male version of Norna. I recognized those same determined eyes and headstrong nature. It must be good to know what you want out of life and in what direction you are bearing.

"If you need anything, let me know," he told me. "You are to meet Dr. Helsley downstairs in the dining room shortly."

What beauty, such rich fabrics and striking rugs! I had gone from the most dismal conditions to the most exceptional. I could not decide which I feared most.

I rinsed off my face and hurried downstairs. I had already kept Dr. Helsley waiting once today. Our dinner consisted of cream of tomato soup, roast beef, boiled potatoes, and a dish that had been created at the hotel, called a Waldorf salad. It was made from apples, celery, walnuts, and mayonnaise over lettuce. It tasted like heaven, certainly a far cry from lukewarm soup and stale bread. For dessert we had fig pudding. I had eaten more at one meal than I had the entire time on the ship.

CHAPTER 13

Dr. Helsley rapped on my door, ordering in a stern voice, "Miss McFadden, do get up. We must not be late for our train."

I looked around, surprised to find that it was already morning. I had been so tired that I had fallen asleep the moment I had felt the softness of the bed. It was not a peaceful sleep, but one filled with fitful dreams. The previous day's activities had proven too much to take in.

I brushed my hands across my dress, smoothing out what wrinkles I could, while berating myself for having been so lax in my actions. I had meant to lay out my dress the night before.

"I will be right there, sir," I answered while opening my valise and checking its contents, not that I thought anything missing. It was just something to steady my nervous hands for the moment.

Once we were on the street, Dr. Helsley took the back of my arm and began directing me toward the train station. The fact that Dr. Helsley did not offer to carry my one small bag made me think him even more offensive than before.

Dr. Helsley walked with such a hurried gait I practically had to run to keep up. I tried to get answers, but he kept rattling on about so much to do and so little time. It seemed as if he was more comfortable giving orders than he was at carrying on a conversation. The more he talked, the more I noticed the preciseness of every word and how he gestured continuously. He kept flinging his small black bag back and forth between his hands. Could he not talk without moving his hands?

When I tried to ask Dr. Helsley about the kind of work that he expected me to do, I only received grunts and head shakes. He seemed to be avoiding the subject entirely. Regardless of my future duties, I was ready to see America, ready to free myself of all the lies and prejudice that had surrounded me at home. Still, I longed to know what was expected of me in my new yet unnamed position.

As we boarded the train, Dr. Helsley informed me that I would be permitted to enter all the cars, including the parlor car. Unlike my steerage ticket on the ship, this ticket was first class. It seemed that since arriving in America, I had suddenly become worth more. Maybe America had given me a bit of luck.

Out of habit, I wrapped my arms around myself, surprised to find that I did not feel the icy grip of guilt. I was now even more excited to see everything America had to offer. It truly was the land of opportunity. Well, so far at least.

The train was nearly full. Dr. Helsley, however, had managed to get us a compartment to ourselves. I would have liked to have shared one. I wanted to meet more Americans.

As Dr. Helsley napped, I decided to see as much of the train as possible and maybe have the chance to talk to someone. The train offered an entirely different look at life from that of the ship. I entered the parlor car and was astonished at the rosewood paneling and deep, comfortable seats of plush burgundy. I had only ridden on a train once, before my trip to America, but that train was not nearly as striking inside. It had been barren and crowded, containing no luxuries, only wooden benches and dirty metal walls.

CHAPTER 14

A fter spending the morning exploring and listening to conversations I longed to join, the conductor announced that lunch was being served in the dining car. A friendly Negro porter with the most charming smile escorted me there.

I was unsure as to whether it was proper to eat alone, but decided that I did not care. Dr. Helsley would find me if he needed me. Unlike the night before in which Dr. Helsley ordered my dinner, the waiter did not order for me. I carefully studied the menu and since I had not had breakfast, I ordered baked eggs topped with cream and buttered crumbs with a cup of coffee.

I picked up a newspaper lying on the table and began reading. It was *The New York Times.* So much was going on in the big city and the world. This was surely the kind of newspaper that Norna would write for.

A young man came by, sat next to me, leaned over, and said, "I never miss an edition, Miss. It's the greatest newspaper on earth. Did you know the first edition was published September 18, 1851? Exciting, isn't it? My father works for the paper."

47

"It is," was all I could say. I was dumbstruck at the thought that someone had actually spoken to me.

The young man hopped up as quickly as he had sat down and was gone. I wondered if he went around quoting dates to all the girls he met. No matter. I had missed my chance at conversation.

I made my way back to Dr. Helsley and sat directly across from him. He did not seem to have been looking for me. How I hoped Norna succeeded in New York! My mind kept drifting back to the voyage. Thoughts of Miriam and Norna comforted me. In all my time in Scotland, I had never felt as close to anyone as I had those two, and in such a short time.

Every so often, the train would jolt and bring me back to the present. Before stopping at a major station, the conductor called out the name of the town. Old faces left the train, while new faces appeared. Each time we stopped, the conductor tore off a perforated section of my ticket and said the same thing: "Miss, could I please see your ticket again? Thank you and have a good trip." The whistle resounded, the train picked up speed, and off we went again.

As I drifted back to thinking of Norna, I lay my head against the window and tried to determine the direction we were heading. The mountains were splendid with traces of powdered snow scattered down their slopes. Such breathtaking scenery!

Sadly, the farther we traveled, the more desolate the scenery became. We passed mountain after mountain, rarely seeing signs of life or civilization. The barrenness made me a little homesick. I was glad to be away from the past, yet I could not help but yearn for a familiar landmark. I missed seeing the rugged and irregular cliffs of Scotland scattered with shepherds overseeing their flocks. And though I enjoyed listening to all the hurried conversations and loud laughter, I missed the Scottish brogue that was my own.

Although Dr. Helsley was sitting quietly and obviously did not want to be interrupted, I felt I had to try once again to find some answers.

"Could you tell me where we are going, Dr. Helsley?"

"We are going to the state of West Virginia."

I hesitated for a moment. "And where might I ask is West Virginia located?"

"It is south of here."

Clearly, I was not going to get anywhere with Dr. Helsley, and not because he was a man of few words. He seemed to be relishing the fact that he had the upper hand.

I resigned myself to the fact that I would have to wait and see what was in store. I loathed living with the unknown, but at the moment I did not seem to have any other option.

CHAPTER 15

The train slowed and jolted to yet another stop. "We have arrived, Miss McFadden," Dr. Helsley informed me as the train pulled into the station.

I peered out the window and read the weathered sign, "Welcome to Mountain Springs."

Such a peculiar name for a town. I looked around to see only one tall, broad-shouldered man, who was standing in a buggy waving his hand toward the train as if he were trying to stop it himself. As soon as the train came to a complete stop, he bounded out of the buggy and raced toward us, talking relentlessly as he reached out with large calloused hands for our bags.

"You must be Miss McFadden. Glad to have you. We've been looking forward to your arrival."

He looked me straight in the eye when he spoke, and I felt a gentleness, which set me instantly at ease. I liked this man whose voice echoed a little too much sorrow.

"You may call me Isobel."

"I am afraid not, Miss McFadden." Dr. Helsley interrupted. "The employees are called by their surnames."

"Employees of what, exactly? When is someone going to tell me what I have been hired to do?" My curiosity, along with my anger, was growing stronger with each passing moment.

"May I ask your name, sir?" I hoped he would tell me both his first and last names, because regardless of Dr. Helsley's rules, I planned to call him by the name I felt most comfortable with.

"My name is Lonzo, Lonzo Crump."

"Well I am glad to meet you, Mr. Crump." I gave a little wink, letting him know that I would be a friend as well as an employee. I hoped my intuition that I could trust this man was correct. I had encountered many men in the pub and acquired quite a talent for reading faces.

I glanced toward Dr. Helsley, seeing that he was much too caught up in himself and his authority to notice the wink.

Mr. Crump tossed our bags into the back of the buggy, smiled, and held out his hand to help me up.

I was wrong to consider Mountain Springs a town. It merely consisted of the train station and a small store with two rooms above it, where we were to spend the night, Dr. Helsley in one room and myself in the other. I did not know where Mr. Crump was to sleep.

CHAPTER 16

W e woke early and had a hurried bite to eat at a table in the corner of the dry goods store. I would hardly have called it a meal. We were then on our way. The trail was long and at times the road seemed impassable. Though I had attempted sleep the night before, worries denied me rest.

We seemed to travel for days rather than hours. Food was not even mentioned. Darkness began to set in, and I found my spirits plunging deeper into despair. This place called West Virginia was so mountainous and the forest so thick that it felt completely cut off from the rest of the world. We had seen neither a house nor a person since leaving the train station. The wind had turned raw and boisterous as we climbed in elevation. The desolation was overwhelming.

"No need to fret, Miss McFadden, we are almost there."

Before I could ask Mr. Crump where *there* was exactly, I saw it. The sun was setting directly behind a monstrosity of a house, if it could be called a house. Perched upon a cliff beside a mountain, the house appeared green, but as we approached, I saw that it was actually enveloped in a rich growth of ivy. There was something indescribably unnerving about that.

A large front porch and massive columns supported the three-story structure. It had to be the most dismal and sinister looking place I had ever seen. The grounds surrounding the house were well kept. However, they appeared as dreary and foreboding as the house.

It was not until we had pulled up closer that I noticed something I had overlooked before. There were bars on all the windows. Could this be a prison? My curiosity turned into fear.

"Mr. Crump, jump out and get the gate," Dr. Helsley bellowed.

"Yes, sir," answered Lonzo Crump, as he smiled toward me.

If Mr. Crump was trying to put me at ease it did not work. I was glad to know he would be around, but no less afraid.

We entered through an iron archway. As I stared at the design of the ironwork, I could not help but notice the words Helsley House Insane Asylum inscribed across the top. I had once overheard a customer at the pub saying that his sister had been sent away to an insane asylum because she was touched in the head. Was this a horrible joke my father had played on me? Had I come here on the pretense of a job when, in fact, I was to be committed? Dr. Helsley must have seen the alarm come across my face.

"You have nothing to fear here. You have been hired as an employee of Helsley House. You are to serve as a matron. I will tell you now that there are forty-two women residing at Helsley House, all of whom are the better class of the female insane," Dr. Helsley informed me. "Paupers, physically diseased women, and convicts are excluded from my asylum. This should do away with any uncertainties you may have. You will be in charge of every aspect of these women's lives. Tomorrow you will be instructed as to what precisely this entails. Your father assured me that you were very capable and would be most efficient at this job."

CHAPTER 17

What had my father done? How could he tell such lies? My mind was the farthest thing from at ease. Before I could think of a reply to Dr. Helsley, the front door opened, and we were greeted by the oldest woman I had ever seen.

"Thank you, Mrs. Polston. Could you please show Miss McFadden to her room?" Dr. Helsley demanded more than requested. He had quite the habit for that.

"We will continue our conversation in the morning." Dr. Helsley waved me off with a flip of his hand.

Although I was more frightened than I had ever been before, I refused to give in to my fears. I followed the ancient Mrs. Polston across the room feeling anxious and confused. Maybe this was my punishment. My father had always assured me that I would one day pay for what I had done.

Mrs. Polston and I ascended two lengthy flights of stairs and proceeded down a long hallway to the end. I was becoming lightheaded and my legs felt weak. I needed to sit down. I did not know if it was from lack of food or from this place.

"Here's your room," Mrs. Polston said. "Breakfast is at seven. I have to attend to matters now."

She was out the door before I could say more than, "Thank you."

I hoped I said it with more conviction than I felt. I gazed around the cold, bare room, which contained a small bed and a chest of drawers. Not one picture hung on the walls. It reminded me of my room over the pub. I slumped back on the bed and as I brought my hands to my face, I began to cry. What did I know of the insane, other than the fact I had questioned my own sanity more than once?

It was then I heard a scream. At first, I could not tell whether I was hearing or doing the screaming, until it suddenly ended. It was only a matter of seconds before it started again. The shrill and miserable scream caused such a deep chill to overtake me that the hairs on my entire body seemed to rise in response.

I held my ears and prayed for the wrenching noise to stop. I had never heard such sounds of pain and suffering. Was there no way to ease that woman's agony?

Before the thought had much more than crossed my mind, another bout of screaming began and it was then that I realized something horrible. It had not been the same woman each time—only the same terrible torment.

At that moment I realized my life would be very different here, with choices no longer my own. After several deep breaths to calm my nerves I began putting the few things I had into the bureau. In the top drawer I found a pen and paper. That, at least, was a good omen. I thought of Norna.

Now was as good a time as any to get started on a new poem. I wished that I had talked to Norna about my poems, but I was afraid she would ask to read them, and I would have been embarrassed to have had such a great writer read something as simple as what I had written.

This time I would write about madness.

Insanity

The confusion in my head is strong
My skull is but a fence
Holding in such scrambled thoughts
Of days that make no sense

Just as quickly as I jotted down the poem another made its way into my head. As Norna had in steerage, I too thought I would find much here to write about.

Nothing

I know no one
It's all a blur
I cannot feel
No feelings stir

I think I'm crazed
And have no mind
For thoughts I think
Are all in rhyme

CHAPTER 18

"Get up!" Mrs. Polston ordered as she barged through the door. "Dr. Helsley needs to talk to you."

I opened my eyes. Once the confusion faded, I saw that it was the same woman who had met us at the door the night before. She looked even older and more miserable in the light of day. Her name was embroidered on her dress—Creasie Polston.

Her hair was gray and wound tightly in a bun. What may have once been smooth and lovely skin now looked like the worn leather of a well-used saddle. Her voice was scratchy and grating. As she spoke, she looked in my direction with jerky, nervous glances.

"I said, get up. Dr. Helsley hasn't got all day."

"Excuse me." I quickly jumped up. "Will breakfast be served soon?"

"Breakfast?" Mrs. Polston's laugh was even more rasping than her voice. "You slept through breakfast. It was an hour ago. Here's your uniform. Now get dressed in a hurry. Dr. Helsley doesn't like to be kept waiting."

Except for the quick bite at the goods store, this was the second day in a row I had gone without food. At least at home I never missed a meal.

The hallway was not much lighter than it had been the night before. Doors lined either side where voices emanated from deep within. It was then I remembered the terrible screams.

As I opened my mouth to ask about what I heard, Mrs. Polston began knocking on a door bearing Dr. Helsley's name in large dark letters.

"Please enter," announced Dr. Helsley. "Have a seat, Miss McFadden. You may go, Mrs. Polston."

Dr. Helsley's office was a great deal more handsomely decorated than anything else I had seen in Helsley House thus far. It had lush white carpet and rose-papered walls with deep, rich-colored walnut furniture. A large window directly behind Dr. Helsley's desk provided a most magnificent view of the mountains. I felt almost an air of normalcy to the room, whatever normalcy might mean.

As I looked around the room, a poem formed in my mind. I did not always know where the words originated, or how they came to be, I just knew they had to be written.

Wallpaper

Roses with those big old eyes
Looking back at me
All around on every wall
Please come and set me free

Roses with your pretty color
Take me far away
To a hillside far from here
With smells of sweetened hay

CHAPTER 19

I had to get control of myself. I did not want to appear weak to Dr. Helsley. An urn of fresh cut flowers sat on the desk directly in front of me. I closed my eyes and for a moment imagined that I was once again home in Maggie Sullivan's garden. I could see her on her hands and knees among her flowers, holding one hand up to shield her eyes from the sun, waving me over with the other hand. When I opened my eyes, Dr. Helsley was looking at me oddly, as if he thought me foolish.

"Dr. Helsley, I am quite hungry and Mrs. Polston informed me that I overslept and missed breakfast. Am I an employee or a prisoner?" I knew that I had spoken boldly, but I had convinced myself that if I did not, then I would, in fact, be a prisoner.

"In the first place you are in no situation to be demanding anything. If you will control yourself, I will explain your purpose here. You are indeed an employee, but employees must follow the rules, as well. The reputation of this establishment is based on its rules and orderliness. You will conform to the rules of Helsley House. Do you understand?"

"Yes, sir," I answered, rather embarrassed.

"I am most pleased to see that you have decided to exhibit some manners. It will make things easier. As I told you last night, you have been hired as a matron. In fact, you will become head matron. Mrs. Polston has been holding down the position until you arrived. She is much too old for the job herself. Once you are trained, Mrs. Polston will work in the kitchen with Mrs. Leota Hayes. She will, however, be of help to you when needed. I am the medical superintendent and owner of this house."

"Dr. Helsley, I am afraid my father has misled you a wee bit. I have no idea how to be a matron of anything, much less an asylum. I must ask you to release me at once."

"I am sorry, Miss McFadden, but I sent money to your father for your first year's wages. I was extremely generous in doing so. There will be no release."

"You have been extremely generous to my father, but I owe you nothing. I have seen no money and my father never told me anything of this debt."

I would have called Dr. Helsley a liar, but this was something I felt sure my father had done. I could do nothing. I had no money and no idea where I was. If I left, Dr. Helsley would most likely call the authorities and report me for the money that had exchanged hands between my father and him. Tears welled up in my eyes, but I refused to let this man see me cry.

"It seems as if you have the upper hand, Dr. Helsley, but I cannot promise you what my father already has. I will work hard and do my best, but again I know nothing of what you have hired me to do." My father had wanted to rid himself of me and had accomplished this quite to his advantage.

"I not only paid Mr. McFadden your first year's salary, which I must say again was taking quite a risk, but I paid him enough for a first class ticket for your travels. I wanted to ensure that you would arrive in good health."

My father had pocketed that money, as well. He had taken the difference between a first class ticket and the ticket for steerage. "I must say again, Dr. Helsley, that my father has withheld the truth from both of us."

"Well, what is done is done. From what I have heard of your father and the fact that he sent you here, I have decided that whatever fate awaits you at Helsley House can be no worse than your fate at home. I am sure you underestimate yourself, Miss McFadden. You are a woman, a young one I admit; but still, you must understand a woman's needs. That is the most important requirement for the job. For the next two weeks you will be trained by Mrs. Polston before she begins working in the kitchen."

"Two weeks!" I could feel my face flushing. "I would need two lifetimes to prepare for something like Helsley House." The only thing in life I had been prepared for was serving ale to a roomful of drunkards. I knew more of men's needs than of women's.

Dr. Helsley had been correct in assuming that my life had not been a grand one, but I doubted he was correct in assuming this one would be better. As the feeling of isolation began to creep into my thoughts so did another poem.

Solitude

Aloneness is a shadow dark
That overlooks us all
It touches each to leave its mark
Of terror on the wall

Dr. Helsley rang a bell and Mrs. Polston entered almost immediately.

"Mrs. Polston, escort Miss McFadden back to her room," Dr. Helsley barked. "And Miss McFadden, do something about that hair of yours."

Hearing the way Dr. Helsley constantly spoke confirmed my assumption that he was more comfortable in giving orders than carrying on a conversation. It seemed he felt too important to be bothered by idle talk with the staff.

As I returned to my room, tears began to fall. No need to stop them now. I retrieved my pen and paper from the drawer and wrote yet another poem.

A Tear

I feel my chin and on it sits
A tear so wet and free
It comes to play upon my face
And comfort only me

My loneliness could make me hard
And fill my life with fears
But when I'm cold and all alone
My friend always appears

For without it I have no one
On whom I can depend
I only know my tear will come
And be my only friend

A body does not have to be
My only kind of friend
For if I could not trust my tear
I'd will my life to end

PART TWO

HELSLEY HOUSE, 1896–1906

CHAPTER 20

I was no closer to being a stern, harsh-faced woman in starched uniform and stout shoes than I had been upon my arrival. I had worked as head matron of Helsley House for nearly a year and felt no more apt at the position than when I began.

Every aspect of my life revolved around my job. It consisted solely of living at Helsley House. With no one to relieve me of my duties, I had not a moment of freedom. I began to question who the fences and locks were really intended for.

I was not only in charge of the women's interests and welfare, but I was the housekeeper as well. Mrs. Polston became sick with pneumonia and died less than two months after my arrival; surely Dr. Helsley knew she was ill before he hired me.

In those two months I had found that Creasie (I called all the staff by their first name when Dr. Helsley was not around), was not as awful as I had first thought, merely a lonely old woman who led a hard life. I actually grew fond of Creasie, and felt a real loss when she died.

It had been Creasie who helped me understand more about the place.

After my first week at Helsley House, Creasie heard me crying.

"Why is Dr. Helsley so harsh? These women, the staff, none of us deserve the wrath he brings down on us. Why does he hate us so? Why does he seem to hate the world?" I asked Creasie questions just as I had Miriam the year before.

"Dear, we are all made up of our past," Creasie said. "There are as many worlds as there are minds in it. What one person sees as bad, another sees as pitiful, and yet another sees as good. There are no simple answers. I don't know if it will help, but let me tell you the story of Dr. Helsley's past." And with that, Creasie began to unravel the story of the man I detested.

"Dr. Helsley's father, Richard, was a rich man. He and his wife, Helen, came over from England around 1840. He hired a number of men to mine the mountains and build this atrocity of a house. As he became even richer, he and his wife kept to themselves more and more until eventually they rarely left the house.

"During the Civil War, Mr. Helsley was good to the soldiers from both the North and the South. He treated them all the same. He became known for saying, 'A man is a man first, and a soldier second.' I always thought kindly of him for that, but not so kindly for how he treated his wife. For all the kindness he had showed others, Mr. Helsley was as equally cruel to his wife."

Creasie took a deep breath and proceeded. "Mrs. Helsley was a nervous type and the fear of helping the soldiers made her even more so. But she kept quiet and never dared upset her husband.

"Mrs. Helsley was already in her late thirties when their son, William, was born. Dr. Helsley was their only child. It had been a hard pregnancy, but not as hard as being a mother proved to be. The more time she spent with the child, the more she complained of headaches, exhaustion, and an overwhelming sense of inadequacy.

"Nothing I said to Mrs. Helsley eased her. She would cry and beg me to help her, saying, 'I swear I love William and want to be a good mother, I just cannot. He simply will not let me. Please help me. Oh, Creasie, I fear what the future holds for us all.'"

Creasie shifted her body. "I tried to calm her mind. I tried to explain to her that none of us knows what the future holds. My own momma had always told me that worrying was like putting money down on something you never really owned.

"Mr. Helsley was at a loss with his wife. Instead of giving her sympathy and some help with their son, he condemned Mrs. Helsley's every move." Creasie frowned and her hands shook. "Eventually, Mr. Helsley brought in a doctor from Brooklyn, New York. He said he was a doctor of the brain and that he studied the mind. His name was Dr. Powell.

"Dr. Powell made his diagnosis immediately and was gone. His opinion was that Mrs. Helsley suffered from a type of melancholy. He suggested that she be kept quiet and away from the child until these feelings passed.

"He gave Mr. Helsley a prescription for his wife, but I always thought the medicine only made her worse. She would just sit and stare out the window for hours at a time. That is when I completely took over the care of the house and the cooking."

Creasie sighed. "Time passed, but nothing changed. When I think back, I don't believe it was all Mrs. Helsley's mind. With Mr. Helsley's cruel criticisms and the medicine, she just never returned to herself.

"The boy was eventually as cruel to his mother as his father was, taunting her in the same ways. I think she couldn't love him, because he wouldn't let her," Creasie sighed.

"Creasie, do you need to stop and rest?" I asked for fear that she was becoming too weary to continue.

"No, I'm fine. A little short winded, but I would like to tell it all. You need to hear the story." Creasie said this while patting her forehead with her handkerchief.

69

I think Creasie knew she would not be on this earth long and was equipping me with the knowledge I needed to better understand the circumstances at Helsley House.

Creasie continued. "Dr. Helsley was only ten when he witnessed his mother murder his father. They were seated at the dinner table, when, in a fit of rage, his mother picked up the very knife she was using to cut her meat and ran it clean through the neck of Dr. Helsley's father. The boy saw it all. That, I suppose, is the reason why he treats women the way he does."

"Did you see all this for yourself?" I asked, astounded by what Creasie had just divulged.

"Lord, no. I was away the night it happened. I was visiting my sister who'd been sick. I only know this because it's what the boy told.

"The courts pronounced Mrs. Helsley insane and sentenced her to a life in an asylum. I don't even know where the asylum was. With no relatives to care for him, at the age of ten, Dr. Helsley was sent away to boarding school, and I went back to live with my sister.

"After Dr. Helsley graduated from medical school he returned home. He had the house remodeled and wrote asking me to help him run Helsley House. When he explained his plans, I asked Dr. Helsley why on earth he wanted to open an insane asylum.

"I remember his reply as if it were yesterday. 'Creasie,' he said, 'I will not let my mother remain where she is. Since I am responsible for one crazed woman, I may as well put my time into caring for more. Of course, these women will only come from the most upstanding of families. I would be very grateful if you could be of assistance and come to work for me. I will pay you a handsome salary.'"

Creasie stood up, checked the door, sat back down, and resumed where she had left off. "I accepted his offer of employment. I didn't do it for the money, though; I did it for Mrs. Helsley. I liked her and over the years I had come to believe nothing about her life seemed right. Dr. Helsley moved his mother here along with me, Lonzo, Leota, and over twenty women who were considered deranged. Since then he has doubled the number of women.

"Dr. Helsley opened Helsley House in 1878 and locked his mother up just like he did the other women. I never heard him speak a kind word to her. I know now that Dr. Helsley didn't bring his mother here for any reason other than to avoid the shame of her presence in a public asylum. He did not do it out of love; that I can bet money on.

"His deep resentment and critical words drove his mother into an even deeper state of lethargy. I know he had been hurt and felt abandoned; but if only he had shown a little under-standing or forgiveness, things could have been better. I could see the resentment in his eyes when he looked at his mother. Dr. Helsley locked her up and gave me full control of her. His only directions were for me to pay her no more attention than I did the other women." Creasie's voice began to tremble a little.

"I didn't argue, because I knew it wouldn't have done any good. I quit giving her the medicine and I thought I saw signs that Mrs. Helsley was emerging from the darkness that had enveloped her soul for so many years. She attempted simple conversation and started asking about her son.

"Night after night I would lie in my bed and listen to her cry out for her son. Dr. Helsley never blinked an eye nor shed a tear. His lack of reaction told all. She suffered in exile until she finally died. I will never believe that she was truly mad. She was just a sad, lonely, mistreated lady."

How dreadful the story of Mrs. Helsley made me feel! It was like something in a horror story. How I wished Norna were here to write a story about this. The story of Dr. Helsley's mother confirmed my belief that he was more than just a rude, arrogant man—he was dangerous. From this point on I would be on guard with my actions and my words when I was in his presence.

Creasie scowled. "It is a shame locking the women up. If the women at Helsley House are deranged, then so am I. They are nothing more than sick, disheartened, and mistreated women. I know a few of the women have problems, but I can't see their troubles being any worse than anyone else's. I don't see anything here that a little love and time and comfort couldn't heal.

"No matter what diagnosis each woman received: imbecile, neurotic, moral defective, idiot, possessed, melancholic, or hysterical, many of these women are just weak and tired. Others are here because somebody else benefits from their disappearance.

"I don't see anything deserving of the treatment Dr. Helsley gives them, but who am I, but a decrepit woman and a servant at that?"

I thanked Creasie for sharing the story. It was a tale between two friends and I never forgot the importance of her story and how it shaped what I believed and felt about the women at Helsley House.

It was then I looked out the window and through the bars. I felt myself to be but a tiny sparrow in a large and lonely cage.

A Bird

A bird forever flaps its wings
But never does it fly
Singing songs inside a cage
Its world is but a lie

72

CHAPTER 21

Shortly after Creasie shared her story with me, Dr. Helsley took a trip and brought back a Negro woman named Annie Butler, who he announced would be helping Creasie and me. Creasie died the next week. With Creasie's death came another responsibility at Helsley House: to prepare the women's remains for burial when they passed on. Since my arrival, Creasie was the first death, and I prayed it would be the last. That proved to be a hopeless prayer.

Lonzo served as the gardener, carpenter, painter, grounds-keeper, and whatever else was needed. He was also in charge of making pine boxes and burying the bodies of those who died.

Dr. Helsley's only job upon someone's death was to view the body and sign a death certificate. Oh yes, and to send a letter informing the family, if any family existed.

Creasie's was the first corpse I ever touched. Her skin was cold, and she had turned a pale color of blue, almost the same shade as her eyes. She was heavy and awkward to lift. I wept for myself and the others. I wept for the bleakness of all our lives as much as I did for Creasie.

We committed Creasie's body to the earth on a damp and foggy day. Lonzo, Leota, Annie, and I surrounded Creasie, while Dr. Helsley spoke a few words of life and death and comings and goings, which sounded more like some ridiculous riddle than a eulogy.

If Creasie had not told me the story of their history together, Dr. Helsley's thoughtless words would have left me to believe that she had been no more than a mere servant of a few years.

"We all know how hard death is, but it is part of life and something no one can avoid. Instead of living life in fear of it, one should live life in respect of it." Dr. Helsley continued for several more minutes. Then almost in the same breath, he instructed everyone that work would resume as usual.

"A few words and in the ground they go," Lonzo whispered in my ear. I had not realized he was standing behind me and I do not know which startled me more, his undetected presence or the hint of disgust I thought I detected in the tone of his voice.

It saddened me to know that Creasie had no one she loved to mourn her death. Would it be that way when I died? Would I never find someone who would love me and mourn for me, or ever find comfort in a man's touch?

As we trod from the graveyard to the house I looked up and caught the pale, sorrowful reflections of the women's faces pressed against the glass, scattered amid the many windows. Their faces no longer resembled that of mothers, or wives, or daughters, or sisters; they were only mirror images of living beings, mere ghosts of the past.

I had to hurry back and put on paper what lay so heavy on my heart.

Reflections

Reflections staring back at me
You look so lost and lorn
Wondering why there's none to see
The way your lives are torn

Your faces look with hollow eyes
No tenderness in sight
Replaced instead by horrid lies
Of terrors in the night

CHAPTER 22

"A re you well, Isobel?" Annie's voice betrayed her exhaustion. Work was long and hard, but Annie never complained.

I had grown fond of Annie as quickly as I had Lonzo and was glad that Dr. Helsley had found someone kind and generous to replace Creasie, although I did not think that was his intention.

"I am fine, Annie. I just worry about the women; change affects them so." I felt more angry than sad.

I supposed Annie's age to be around forty, but I had miscalculated more than one woman's age. The brutality of the world aged many beyond their years.

"Annie, how can you always exhibit such cheerfulness? Do you really like it here?" I asked.

"It's not a matter of like or dislike. It's a matter of making the best of where you are and what you have. I could fuss and cry about my life and the unfairness of it all, but what good would that do? It wouldn't help me or anybody else. So I smile, and thank God that I am alive and well."

Her words left me feeling wistful for such a positive outlook. I found myself opening up to Annie before I had a chance to measure my words, just as I had with Norna. There was such a familiarity between Miriam and Creasie, and Norna and Annie.

"I hate to admit it, but I do not know if I believe in God. I believe in luck and that there is a kind of positive and negative energy at work in the world, but it seems I have seen the negative more times than the positive. I suppose that could be the ole Devil and God at odds."

If my words shocked Annie, she never showed it. Instead, she just smiled and continued talking. "Who says what God is exactly? To some he's an old white-haired man sitting on a throne. Some see him white. Some see him black. I bet some even see him as a woman. The world gets awfully heavy at times if you try to carry it all by yourself. Nobody has shoulders that big. I have to believe that things, even painful things, happen for a reason.

"I've seen terrible suffering in my life, Isobel. My parents were slaves and when I was only six years old, I was sold off to another owner. That was the last time I ever saw any of my family." Annie hung her head. "I know how these women feel, being taken away from their families. It is something I would not wish upon any soul."

Annie rubbed the back of her neck before she continued. "My new owners purchased me to do housework and tend to their new baby. The people weren't my family, but they weren't as bad as a lot of slave owners. We had a good president then, Abraham Lincoln. I didn't agree with everything I heard he said and did, but he did try to free the slaves.

"After I got my freedom, I tried to find my parents, but never could. They'd been sold off, too," Annie said. "Many white people in the South didn't believe in freeing their slaves, and kept on hunting and killing the Negroes even after the war ended. Our being free might have been a law, but that didn't stop some people from still thinking we were property.

"I headed up north from Alabama and found my way to a small town named Catlettsburg, over in Kentucky. That's where Dr. Helsley found me. Catlettsburg has two dry goods stores, two grocers, two hardware stores, two warehouses, and one drug store. It's one of the biggest towns I've ever lived in."

"How far is Catlettsburg from here?" I asked.

"I guess it to be about a hundred miles or so from here, give or take a few miles, but through the mountains it might as well be a million."

Annie sat forward and continued. "I never married. I found a good man who was willing to hire a Negro woman to work in his dry goods store and I lived a simple life. I tried to mind my own business and stay out of people's way. I'd seen enough trouble to last a lifetime.

"While I was working at the store, Dr. Helsley came in and asked for the owner. I heard Dr. Helsley introduce himself and ask him if he knew anybody who'd be interested in employment with his establishment, free room and board.

"For some reason I can't explain, it interested me. I learned where Dr. Helsley was staying the night and at supper time while he was eating his meal I got up the nerve to talk to him. I wasn't sure how he would feel about having his meal interrupted, especially by a Negro woman, but I didn't want to go up to his room.

"So I walked right up to him and said, 'Dr. Helsley, sir, my name is Annie Butler and I would be happy if you would consider me for the job I overheard you talking about. I'm a real hard worker and I would do a good job.'"

Annie lowered her voice, "Dr. Helsley asked about my family and when I told him I didn't have any, he hired me right there and then.

"That was the only question he asked me. Not a thing about references, or if I knew anything about what was to be expected of me. I thought about that on the way out here, and almost changed my mind. I started getting worried about the whole thing, but I had already quit my job at the store. So I came ahead. Now, here I am at Helsley House."

"It seems as if Dr. Helsley's main requirement for working for him is the lack of any family ties," I said softly.

"Don't look so sad, Isobel. This job's not so bad. I've seen a lot worse. It just hurts me because these women at Helsley House are just as much slaves as we Negroes were." Annie swallowed hard. "I can't figure why someone always has to own someone else and tell them what to do. Why can't we all just be free and help one another live in a little peace?"

I didn't have an answer for Annie. All I could do was remember my journey to America and what Miriam had said about one person being worth more than another.

It had been a long day and I felt more tired than usual. The women were quiet and had gotten in bed with no outbursts. I was able to escape into my bedroom early and for that I was grateful. I lay quietly in bed, but as much as I tried to sleep, it was to no avail. The old guilt that continued to haunt me materialized. The darkness and silence opened a doorway for its presence to enter through.

I got up and began to write.

The Guilt

For me there is not peace inside
No peace but ugliness
There is too much for me to hide
Or even to confess

For if I tried who would be there
To hear my lonely cry
No one alive would want to share
The burden of my lie

The lie that holds my guilt so tight
To never let me go
The one that holds me close at night
And drags me deep below

This guilt of mine will thrive I fear
If ever do I tell
So written on the paper here
Are secrets in a well

CHAPTER 23

How I wished I could talk to Norna. I had known her for only a short time, but I thought of her as my best friend. Helsley House would have been a perfect location for Norna's stories of misery and sadness.

I thought of trying to leave and find Norna. I still had the address she slipped into my hand before we parted, but I knew Dr. Helsley would never let me go. It was just as well, for I could not bring myself to leave the women.

I would be of no help to anyone if I did not get control of myself and do what was expected of me. Annie was rubbing off on me. I slowly began to realize my need to dwell on the affirmative side of being at Helsley House. It was the first time I had ever been needed by anyone, that was something positive; I could not, and would not allow my wretched father to get the better of me. But as much as I detested him, I could not help wishing for a father who could have loved me.

I began to write, understanding that without my writing I would be destined to a life of uncontrolled emotions.

A Father

A father should be there to hug
Just like a big old bear
And wake his little girl each day
To help her brush her hair

A father should be very strong
And love his little girl
Singing silly songs to her
Then giving her a twirl

A father should be there to soothe
To give a big old kiss
And tell his little girl each night
She'll be the one he'll miss

My father should do all these things
But no, he never does
For in his eyes I've never lived
I'm not the one he loves

I knew from the looks on the women's faces that they cared about me as much as I cared about them. I had come to think of each woman as either the mother or sister I had never had. I would devote myself to their care and listen to the wrenching stories that each of them told in hopes of helping just one of them to feel less pain. I kept thinking of Mrs. Helsley.

CHAPTER 24

"M iss McFadden, I need your help in the treatment room," Dr. Helsley announced through tightly pressed lips as I was helping with the noon meal. I tried to help Annie in the kitchen as much as she helped me with the housekeeping. Leota had simply left the week before without any indication as to why, and had not been heard from since.

Dr. Helsley suddenly entered the kitchen. I hoped he had not overheard Annie and me discussing Leota's possible whereabouts.

Dr. Helsley cleared his throat several times. "I would like to put an end to the gossip and speculation about Mrs. Hayes. She has gone back East to help with her ailing mother, and no one will be hired to replace her. Now continue on with your duties. I do not want to hear any more discussions on this subject." His voice betrayed no emotion.

From that point on, I knew it would be just Annie and me. It would make for longer days, but we made a good pair. One great thing I had found in coming to America was friendship.

Going downstairs to the treatment room was the duty I hated most. The basement was where Dr. Helsley claimed to help his patients overcome their insanity. I was no doctor, but I could see that Dr. Helsley's methods were not helping. He was doing nothing more than experimenting on these poor women. The first time I aided Dr. Helsley in one of his experiments I became physically ill and was reprimanded severely. Eventually, I conditioned myself to assist Dr. Helsley without getting sick. I convinced myself that if I did not help, then Dr. Helsley would find someone who did not sympathize with the women, and that would be much worse.

I followed Dr. Helsley down the stairs. Allison Miller was waiting, her face drained of color. I had found that Allison's madness was nothing more than an expression of her energy and ambition. Allison would not be bullied by anyone to relinquish her beliefs. I thought of the conversation we had shared a short time after my arrival.

"Last night I could feel the warmth against the back of my neck. I knew that it was you, Isobel, holding the lamp above my head to see if I had gone to sleep. Every night since your arrival you have done so. You are a constant comfort, something I did not know before you came." Allison took my hand.

"At night I pretend to sleep, but instead I am reliving my last night at home," Allison said with tears in her eyes. "I do this every night. I keep the pain of what my husband did to me fresh. I must not replace that cold hatred with sorrow or pity for myself. That would surely be the death of me. Hatred will be what surely helps me escape this nightmare and return home to my daughters." Allison's eyes turned from teary to hard. A thin line emerged across her forehead.

"Is that not too much to bear?" I asked. "How difficult that must be on you. Would you like to talk about what happened? I would like to hear your story, Allison." I hoped by sharing my gift of listening, I could relieve some of her distress.

Allison laid her head in my lap and began to tell the story that had brought her to Helsley House. Like Norna, Allison could follow a purpose she believed in to the very end—a determination that many men, especially Allison's husband, feared.

"My husband, Edward, insisted that I was being foolish because I did not believe everything to be the way he believed, and I refused to allow him control over me and our daughters. A father was what our daughters needed, not a dictator.

"I could see the fear in Edward's eyes, but I could also hear the anger in his voice. He demanded that my role in life was to stay at home with our children and take care of the house. He refused to listen to my ideas of working outside the home.

"I pleaded for him to listen to me. I let him know that I thought it wrong not to allow me to better myself, and to teach our daughters to accept less than they deserve or want.

"They are strong and smart girls and should be treated as such; not as weak and simple-minded fools that anyone can push around. How dare he want that for them, or for me?

"He continued to beseech me to come to my senses. He declared that what he wanted for me was not only his way but the way of the church. I laughed out loud at the very thought, and told him that the church surely would not put such injustices on women. He did not find that comical.

"He had the audacity to say that God would strike me down for what I believed. I explained that it was not God who would strike me down, but man; a selfish and ruling man who believes me to be less than him."

Allison frowned. "It was then that Edward grabbed a sheet from the bed and wrapped me so tightly I feared that I would die for lack of air. I could not believe that Edward was doing this. He had never laid a hand on me in any way other than with love and kindness. I did not know this man. The church with its new minister had filled his mind with such ideas that it was Edward who had become mad, not me. Edward feared the church and wanted our family to be accepted in the community. I knew then that Edward feared the church more than he loved me.

"Edward insisted that the girls go next door and stay with our neighbor, Mrs. Jenkins. He gave them a kiss and rushed me off to be seen by Dr. Langley.

"The doctor sided with Edward and stated that I was suffering from hysteria. I do not know if it was chloroform or belladonna or both that I was given. When I awoke I was at Helsley House. In spite of my objections and protests, here I have remained. That was almost three years ago and I have not heard from my husband or my daughters since." Allison's eyes filled again.

"Edward's last words will forever be embedded within my mind. 'Allison, when you tell the doctor that you were wrong and that the church was right I'll come back for you, but not a minute before.'"

Allison looked around the room. "I pray each night that my daughters are well and that I will continue to have the strength to hold on until I find a way to get out. Whatever my daughters are going through cannot cause them as much pain as living the rest of their lives by the rules Edward would thrust upon them if allowed."

Allison's story had fueled a fire in my soul. Norna would be proud of Allison's strength.

CHAPTER 25

I returned my thoughts to the present. There was no more pleading in Allison's eyes as we looked at one another. The pleading for me to prevent him had stopped. The women realized that I was in no more of a position to stop Dr. Helsley than they were. I was no different from them.

It would be a cold water bath this time. Dr. Helsley said that a cold water bath calmed nervous irritability and a warm bath eased mania. I had yet to see anything as soothing as a warm bath used. He also performed other procedures such as bleedings, purges, and vomits. Dr. Helsley was not trying to help the women—he was trying to break them.

Each of Allison's sessions with Dr. Helsley found her submerged in ice cold water for nearly an hour. Sometimes when Allison was not physically able to get into the water, she was restrained and wrapped in a sheet that had been soaked in ice water. Her screaming stopped. Allison merely stared as though she had willed herself to another world.

Dr. Helsley immediately left the women in my care after completing his so-called procedures. It was up to me to return them to their rooms.

Dr. Helsley maintained an incredibly structured schedule and I had learned his schedule down to the minute. After helping Allison back to her room, I slipped into Dr. Helsley's office to read until it was time for him to return, which was not nearly as long as I would have liked. Dr. Helsley had a vast library of journals, magazines, newspapers, and books, mostly medical.

I had found documents and articles written about other asylums. Many women who had been neglected or abused found themselves locked away. As bad as conditions were here, some asylums kept women in filth and nakedness, placed in rooms with little ventilation, and given insufficient amounts of food. Some had even been chained. If the women were not mad when they arrived, they would be before they left, although I had yet to see anyone leave Helsley House, other than through the graveyard. I did not understand a world that would allow these injustices. The thought made me shudder.

The latest newspaper Dr. Helsley had received was lying on his desk. He received *The New York Times* every week. I read the newspaper in its entirety, searching every name in print, looking for Norna's. From time to time, it appeared.

I could see that the world was moving right along without me knowing or seeing any of it. Dr. Helsley had circled many articles pertaining to the fight for women's rights, especially the right to vote. There were articles in the paper about it every week. I could tell from the articles that it was fast becoming a strong topic. I also knew it was something Dr. Helsley would fight against.

There were countless numbers of women who had stood up and voiced opinions contrary to those of society. Many of these women were being forced into asylums just like Helsley House. They were made examples of to keep other women in line. Outspoken women, known as *suffragettes*, had become a threat to men.

In the last article I read, I saw what I had been searching for. Norna's name jumped out in black ink, but this time not only had she written an article, but she had been featured in one, as well.

I could hardly believe what I was reading, yet I should not have been surprised by any of it. Norna had been taken to jail for attending a suffragette rally. The article quoted her as saying, "Suffrage is something to fight for, endure, and even die for."

The women of Helsley House were living proof of what Norna was fighting for. I grew up not having a woman in my life to share intimate thoughts and feelings with, and here I was, surrounded by them. How I wished Norna were here to see these gracious women, hear their heartbreaking stories, and become a voice for them. I caught myself wishing this almost daily.

How was I to get past my own feelings of guilt and worry? How could I be of any real use to these women? I went back to my room with great sadness. I could not help but feel useless. I wanted to scream at the injustices surrounding me. Allison being torn from her children merely because she was a vital and strong woman who wanted more for her daughters than what the social order was willing to give. Such dismal circumstances women had to endure.

As I lay down to sleep, I envisioned growing up with the strength of a mother's love and drifted off with a poem engrained in my mind.

Mother

I think about you every night
Through bright clear eyes I see
The way you hold me very tight
Your love to me is free

You do not ask for me to be
A thing that I am not
You only ask I let you see
The love that I have fought

I do not have to act as though
My heart's as tough as nails
The love and warmth I have to show
Can ring as loud as bells

To you I give my love for free
From deep inside my soul
I do not care who else might see
The way you make me whole

CHAPTER 26

In spite of the lengthy days and strenuous work, the time passed quickly at Helsley House. I had grown to think of it as my home and I had acquired relationships I once dreamed of. My father had not gotten the last laugh, to be sure. He may have meant to send me to the depths of hell, but instead, he had given me a reason to be in this world. He had given me the family he denied me in childhood.

At the same time, however, an agony had taken hold that I could not shake. It was as though my heart had abandoned my words, because the things I saw and felt could never be verbalized. I could not forget the importance of pen and paper that Norna stressed. I knew I had to keep writing, keep documenting my feelings in my poems. Seeing the words on paper made the stories and horrors of these women's lives more real. Documenting my thoughts somehow insured that in some small way they would not be forgotten.

Annie tried to help me get away by myself for at least a few minutes a day. I found a kind of peace on the cliff along the side of the house that overlooked the river. It was a barrier

Dr. Helsley hoped would deter the women from trying to flee. There was no need for a barrier; the mountains themselves were more than any woman could conquer.

Sitting on the edge of the cliff looking down into the river provided a kind of release for me. It reminded me of the cliffs of Scotland, making me feel homesick, even though home was a place with few good memories.

Almost four years had passed. I would soon have my twentieth birthday and was thinking of what I would be doing in Scotland as a twenty year old woman; no doubt still serving ale to a drunkard lot of men. When I heard Annie calling my name, I brought myself back to the here and now and raced toward the house in fear that Dr. Helsley was on another rampage. I was not quite sure how I accomplished it, but in the last two years I had stopped cowering and started defending myself. I decided that Norna was not the only one whose voice could make a difference. Although it had not made Dr. Helsley any less brutish, it seemed to earn me a small amount of respect. I had become the mediator between Dr. Helsley and anyone who angered him.

When I approached the front door there stood a wet and terrified girl with a weathered and stubble-faced man pushing her into the arms of Annie.

"Excuse me, sir." I stopped to recover my breath. "May I ask the problem?"

"There's no problem, lady. I have the papers right here."

I took the envelope he pulled out from the inside of his coat and read:

Here is the fee we discussed and a signature from Dr. Lafferty, stating that Callie is not of sound mind and should be committed.

It was without a doubt a legal document certifying that Callie Lynn Crider, age fourteen, was a promiscuous young woman who was to be committed to Helsley House.

How absurd! She was nothing more than a frightened child, who, if promiscuous, needed a firm grip by her parents, not an insane asylum.

Dr. Helsley had clearly heard the commotion. "Miss McFadden, may I see that?" he demanded.

"Everything looks to be in order. Sir, would you please thank Mr. Crider for his immediate action and tell him that Callie will be well cared for." Dr. Helsley's smile chilled me to the bone.

I wanted to laugh out loud. How preposterous, even for Dr. Helsley. Were we now to be taking in committed children?

"Well, I guess I'll be getting back now," the stubble-faced man said, tipping his hat and bowing backwards out the door.

I could see the unease in the man's eyes and knew that he no more agreed with these actions than I did. Before his eyes said too much, he turned quickly and fled.

I took hold of Callie's hands. They were freezing.

CHAPTER 27

Callie must have felt as I did upon my arrival. Confused and scared, nothing more than someone else's property to do with as they wished.

"Miss McFadden, will you take Callie upstairs and get her out of those wet clothes and into something dry?" Dr. Helsley asked, with false sentiment. I will be retiring early tonight.

Once again, I was left to explain the rules. Dr. Helsley had taken to having a sip of brandy in his room in the evening hours and retiring early.

"Please don't let him leave me. I'm not crazy and I don't belong here," Callie begged. "I want my mother."

"I know, Callie, but for now we must go upstairs and get you dried off before you become ill." It was all I dared say. Crossing Dr. Helsley at the wrong time would only make things worse.

I took Callie to a room as close to my own as possible and after removing a most beautiful, but soaked hair ribbon, I quickly dried her hair with a towel and helped her out of her wet clothes. No matter how I tried to console and comfort her, I did nothing more than keep Callie's hysteria at bay. I did so by allowing her to keep her hair ribbon tucked neatly away.

Her eyes were full of questions that I had no answers for. I promised myself that I would protect this child the best I could from the horrors that Dr. Helsley would surely subject her to. How in the world had she ended up here?

Someone surely wanted to rid himself of her as badly as my father had me. That, Callie and I had in common. What would become of either of us?

In only a few days' time, Callie and I became friends. I felt much less than six years her elder. Since coming to America I had become friends with women of all ages: Norna, who was a few years older than me, and now Callie, who was a few years younger, both more of a friend to me than any girl in Scotland my own age had ever been. I wondered if Norna ever thought about me.

Callie reveled in talking about her home. She talked about it with such pride.

"We live in Kentucky on the most magnificent ranch where my family is known for raising the best thoroughbreds around for racing," she boasted. "I even have a colt of my own. I am hoping one day to race him in The Kentucky Derby."

"Even I have heard of The Kentucky Derby," I said.

It was then she bowed her head and began to cry. "Isobel, why has my mother not come for me? I don't understand why I must remain here. She surely does not know what has happened."

"I do not know, Callie. Just remain strong and hopeful that one day she will come." I said, but did not feel it would ever happen. It was not long before the horrible truth of why Callie was at Helsley House finally became clear. I suspected the truth after the third morning of helping Callie back to her room from breakfast as she was overcome with nausea and vomiting. Callie had no inkling as to what I suspected. If not for the knowledge I had obtained from reading Dr. Helsley's books and journals, I do not think I would have known, either.

I sat Callie down and explained my suspicions to her, and I asked if it was possible that she might be with child. Callie began to weep hysterically. I had never felt more sadness for anyone in my whole life, not even myself.

I told Callie that everything would be fine, knowing in my heart that it would not be. Callie needed a friend now more than she needed the truth.

"I cannot have a baby. It will be a monster. You don't understand. Just take it out, do you hear me, take it out!" Callie cried hysterically.

"Callie, listen to me. Get control of yourself and calm down. I know this is a shock, but if Dr. Helsley hears you, it will not be good. I have protected you so far, but there is much here you have not seen. You must stay calm. You cannot simply take a baby out. It does not work that way. You must be quiet about this for now and let me decide how to tell Dr. Helsley."

"You don't understand Isobel, I cannot have this baby."

"You can, Callie. I will be here to help you. I am not sure how just yet, but I will convince Dr. Helsley that the baby must remain with you until I can think of a plan."

"No, Isobel, I don't want this baby to remain with me. I don't want this baby at all. It will be a monster, I tell you. I know it will."

Her insistence that she *could* not have the baby baffled me. I knew she was young, but many young girls dream of being a mother long before they are ready, the thoughts of holding and coddling such a small and helpless creature and of having someone to love them overshadowing reality. Unfortunately, the girls seldom realized how much work a baby would be.

"You don't know the horrible truth, Isobel. I cannot even speak it. It is more ghastly than anything you could imagine."

"It is all right. Please tell me. I will not reject you or think less of you. I love you, Callie. Our friendship is stronger than that. Now tell me."

I took hold of Callie's hands and held them to my chest. "What is it that agitates you so?"

"The baby. How can I even say this aloud? The baby belongs to my father," Callie wailed.

The shock on my face must have frightened her, for she began to cry convulsively.

"Callie, you must stop crying. I was only shocked, no more. It is not your fault. Do you understand?"

The stories of what happened when a baby was born to those closely related was common knowledge; babies were born with deformed limbs and retarded minds. Not only did Callie have to face the stigma of bearing her own father's child, but the child could be defective. I would not have had her strength in such a dilemma.

As deplorable as the situation was, it was not unheard of. Over the last year I had heard other women's stories of the terrible acts that had been committed upon them by their fathers, brothers, uncles, and even sons. This was more heartbreaking than unheard of for I had known such goings-on existed long before coming to Helsley House. I had even written a poem about this very thing.

Night Wings

Each of them was but a child
Forced into sinful things
Growing up alone and wild
Dressed in worldly wings

Wings that flew them through the night
Into the arms of men
And brought them back before the light
To be alone again

Wings that hid all of the lies
So none could see the pain
That lingered deep beneath soft cries
Where loneliness remained

CHAPTER 28

G rowing up working alongside my father in a vile and nasty pub filled with smoke and vermin, I knew the wickedness men could inflict. Though my own father did not, there were men there that would bed their own daughters as quickly as their friends' daughters. I had heard more than one of them brag about it. I did not even try to explain men such as these to Callie. My words would have fallen upon deaf ears.

Callie grew more distant with each passing day. I could hardly get her to talk and she could not bring herself to look me in the eyes. The shame Callie carried was far more obvious than the baby.

Callie had withdrawn into herself, her face drawn and her countenance far from strong. If Callie could have willed her own death, I was sure she would have. She had accepted her father's sins as her own and resigned herself to the worst. As hard as I tried, I could not make her see the situation in any other light.

Though she weighed almost as much as I did, I sat her on my lap and smoothed her hair. "Callie, it was not your fault. You are his child, his daughter. No matter what you did—and

I do not think you did anything at all—it was not your fault. You did not even do it. He did. He was the adult and should have controlled his feelings. He was supposed to protect you, not hurt you. He should be ashamed, not you."

I was not only trying to convince Callie of what I was saying, but myself as well. My own father had not treated me as awfully physically, but he had, mentally. I continued, "Do not let him off so easily by taking his shame."

"I did not fight him hard enough. It had been so long since he comforted me. At first, I liked the warmth of his touch, but as a father's touch only, nothing more. It was my fault," Callie cried.

The pain her eyes revealed was almost more than I could bear. As much as I wanted her to forget everything that had happened, I knew that she could not. She had to remember and defeat these awful memories. Only by overcoming the past could she find the strength to go on. That I had learned from the women.

"Tell me, Callie, exactly how it happened."

Callie recoiled. "I cannot bear to tell you such awful things. I cannot."

"Listen to me, Callie. Every woman in this place has had horrible things done to them. Would you blame any of it on them? You can see the pain in their eyes. It may not be worse than yours, but it is pain, all the same. They have shared their stories with me in hopes that it would somehow keep those memories from growing and festering inside them. Please tell me, Callie. I would never judge or find fault with you. I love you, Callie."

CHAPTER 29

I will tell you, Isobel, but it will not be easy. This is the truth, I promise."

"I will believe whatever you tell. Go ahead, Callie. Take your time."

Callie rose from my lap and lay on the bed. As her story began, her eyes focused on the ceiling. She refused to look at me.

"The times I had been held and loved by my father had long since passed. When he gave me Jameson, my colt, I thought he had changed. I thought he was starting to love me again. But I think he only gave me the colt to give me a reason to be in the barn. That's where it happened." Callie's expression was solemn.

"Every night, I would go out and check on Jameson before going to bed. Mama said it was a good idea for me to have something of my very own to love.

"One night my father came to the barn, and I could smell his breath. He had been drinking more and more. He talked about how much I was starting to look like my mother, and that I was becoming 'quite the looker.' He came over and sat down next to Jameson and me and started going on about what a good job I was doing. I had not been complimented by my father in such a long time." Callie's voice faltered. "He started to twist my braids and make jokes and I liked it. I did not like his breath, but I liked the attention he was giving me. I had not laughed with him in a long time and so I didn't stop him."

Callie's breathing quickened, but I pressed her to continue.

"The next thing I knew he was laying on top of me pulling at my dress. I tried to get him to stop. I begged him, but he kept calling me Lynette, as if he thought I was Mama. He was too heavy to push away. After he finished, it was then I saw his eyes. It was as if he had just realized who I was. He jumped up and told me to get in the house and the next time I tried something like that he was going to give me the whipping of my life. It happened two more times. Each time I tiptoed back to the house, so ashamed, afraid to tell Mama. I did not want to hurt her. I was afraid she would blame me.

"It was about a month after the last time my father touched me that he came to my bedroom late one night to wake me. He told me to hurry and get dressed and meet him outside. He explained that Jameson had been hurt and he didn't want to wake my mama and worry her.

"I quickly jumped up and got dressed," Callie said. "My father was standing outside with the horses saddled and ready to go. I couldn't understand how he could have known about Jameson, since it was the middle of the night and he should have been in bed. But all I cared about was Jameson.

"I was so worried that Jameson might be hurt. I loved him more than anything in the whole world, perhaps even more than my parents. That wouldn't be saying a lot about my father," Callie said. "It was as if I was more a bother than a person."

"As my father and I crossed the creek on the horses, I started wondering why Jameson was so far from the house instead of in the barn. Then I heard whistles. From behind a tree came a man I had never seen before. He wore his hat low over his forehead. He asked my father if he had the girl and the money and said, 'I don't have all night.'"

"I thought he had mistaken us for people he knew. Before I could ask my father, I had my answer.

"My father yelled at the man and told him to shut up and keep his part of the bargain; which meant keeping his mouth shut, too.

"Before I could make a move, the man covered my head with a grass sack and dragged me off one horse and threw me over the back of another." Callie squeezed her eyes shut. "I heard my father's horse turn and ride the other way.

"But where was Jameson? Who was this man? How did my father know him? The questions were making my head spin. I was trying hard not to think about the awful things I knew I should be feeling.

"The grass sack remained over my head until I had no idea where I was or how long we had been riding. We rode during the day and stopped and slept on the ground for three more nights."

Callie wrinkled her nose. "He smelled, and I could tell that he was near me even when I could not see him. I asked him where he was taking me, but he would only laugh and say that he was taking me where he was getting paid to take me.

"I could not imagine where that might be, so I asked him again. He only said that he wasn't supposed to answer any of my questions, so for me to be quiet and not talk until he dropped me off. He said that I could scream to the high heavens then, because it wouldn't do me a bit of good. It would probably prove my father right.

"I could not imagine what my father had been *right* about. I asked him again what was happening.

"He just shook his head and wouldn't answer me. I had no idea what to think." Callie looked stunned all over again. "I had never spent a single night away from home. Before I knew it, I was jerked off the horse.

"He shouted for me to get up and when I did not, I felt his hands scoop me up as if I were a baby. It started raining and my dress and stockings were muddy and cold.

"He knocked on your door and delivered me here. Now I am glad I did not know where I was going." Callie shuddered as she stood up and went to the window. She placed her elbows on the sill of the window and stared out into the night. I, too, stared into the night as the words of a poem whisked through my mind.

Within

He came into the barn that night
She smelled his drunken breath
She knew it that it was going to be
A fate much worse than death

The words he spoke were that of ice
His heart as cold as stone
He did not see her as a child
But as a woman grown

She thought she should have screamed and fought
Or found someone to tell
So now to God she'll pay the price
She fears the threat of hell

CHAPTER 30

Callie would not allow herself a hint of relief. I did not understand the workings of the mind. How could Callie excuse the very man who had disgraced her? How could Callie blame herself? But had I not taken the blame for my own father's actions? Had I not always wondered what I could have done to make my own father hate me? Did I not feel overwhelmed with guilt?

The mind is a strange thing. No matter what I said, Callie had made up her mind to condemn herself, believing that she did belong in this place.

"Callie, I do not seem to have the words to comfort, to console you. Even though there is nothing to forgive, only when you can forgive yourself can you find peace," I said as my lower lip trembled. I was giving advice that I had not heeded myself.

I began forming another poem within my mind. As hard as I had tried to convince Callie the importance of writing her thoughts down, whether it be in poetry or in a diary, she would hear nothing of it.

Unloved

I had no one to understand
My problems and my fears
That greeted me along the way
And added up with years

I only wanted to be loved
Someone to trust and hold
But when I cared, he turned away
His heart was icy cold

He knew that I was all alone
With no one by my side
Replacing love with shame and guilt
He stole my trust and pride

I felt I owed a great deal to Callie, who had helped me see
how wrong my own father had been, and that I was not to
blame for his hatred.

It was then I decided to tell Callie the truth of my father, and
how I too, in a much different way had suffered. I prayed that
Callie would listen and hear what I was telling her. I prayed she
would come to her senses.

CHAPTER 31

I helped Callie back into bed and pulled the cover up to her chin. She might not listen, but that would not stop me from trying. I began telling my story.

"My father was from a highland village in Scotland called Rosemarkie. It was a quaint little fishing village on the Southeast shore of the Black Isle. It had a beautiful beach and the steepest of cliffs. My father and his father before him were fishermen. It was a story I had heard my father tell to others many times." I took a deep breath and continued.

"From the stories my father told, I pieced together that my mother was from somewhere near Rosemarkie, but I do not know exactly where. I am not even sure how they met. If not for my father's drunken outbursts I would have known nothing about their life together.

"When my father took to ale, he rattled and talked on about their meeting, how they fell in love and about the lives they led together; but no matter how drunk he was, he would always look up and see me standing there and curse the day I was born. He never missed an opportunity to tell me how I would pay for what I had taken from him, for killing my mother." I could hear my voice rising as I spoke. "For all my sins."

"My father swore that he would take all that was good from me, as I had him. I never grieved for the mother I never knew. I was too filled with guilt for having killed her.

"I was so filled with remorse that at times I could not take a breath for fear I might breathe air that someone else needed more. This consumed me and every aspect of my life."

I continued as memories came flooding back.

"My grandmother Margaret, my father's mother, lived with us until she died of pneumonia when I was four years of age. I do not remember much about her, only that it was the only time in my life I felt taken care of. I heard my father curse her in more than one drunken rage. If not for my grandmother, I think my father would have placed me in a sack and thrown me in the river like a stray cat. After she died, my father moved us from Glasgow to Edinburgh. There he was hired to work in a pub and as I got older he found use for me. I may have been young but I worked hard. I worked for the approval he never seemed able to give.

"My mother's mother, Agnes, came to visit when I was seven years of age. She said it had taken her that many years to find us. She tried to tell me about my mother but my father would not hear of it.

"My father shouted that she told only lies. It was the only time I ever saw her. My father said she had suffered a heart attack and died right after that. I do not know if that was the truth or not. I never knew either of my grandfathers. They had both passed on before I was born."

I stopped my story for a moment and looked closely at the sadness that filled Callie's eyes. I did not know if I was hurting or helping, yet I continued.

After my arrival at Helsley House I found a letter hidden tightly away inside a dress pocket. I was only sixteen at the time. My father had placed it there before I left home. I have read it so many times that it will forever be stained upon my heart.

"He called me by name and said I was nothing more than a witch. He blamed me for my mother's death and damned me to hell. He had even named me after Isobel Gowdie, the queen of Scottish witches. He said that I like Isobel Gowdie, had made a pact with the devil and could transform myself into any creature I wanted. That I could become a cat and scratch his eyes out if I wanted.

"He swore that I drew out the last breath of my mother when I sucked in my first breath. It was then he cast me out and sent me to America.

"I was a child without a mother, only a father who hated me; who blamed me for killing my own mother.

"As a child, I heard the stories of witches, and banshees, and fairies. They were the beliefs of many, a way of life in Scotland. But never had I thought of them as anything more than a tale to entertain a child. How could my own father believe such things to be true? How could he believe me to be a witch?" I gasped as if it were a new thought.

"To bring such wrath upon an innocent child, my father should be the one locked away somewhere. His letter did not anger me. It brought relief. I had always known my mother died in childbirth and that my father blamed me and hated me for that. I just felt there was something more I had done besides, something so terrible that no one could speak of it. To find out that it had been nothing more than the mere fact that I had been born! Something I had no control of. I was astonished. Nothing I could have done would have changed anything." I felt the anger rise.

"I know now that it was my father who was evil. Not me. That is easy to see now, but not to a child who is naïve and believes what she is told. It is not easy to overcome feelings of shame and fear. My mind may say now that it is time to put it away, but my heart does not know how. I will learn, just as you must learn.

"I will not allow my father to have one more drop of my heart or my innocence to crush beneath his feet. Just as you, Callie, must give no more of yours."

As the words to a poem took shape within my mind I secretly thanked Norna for assuring me that writing was a good thing for the soul. If only Callie could believe that.

A Heart

He took my heart so selfishly
A man he had to feel
He used my heart as if his own
As though he did not steal

My heart he took for his own strength
In hopes to have control
By being stronger than myself
He made himself feel whole

CHAPTER 32

Telling the story brought back all the misplaced guilt that had thrived in me. How I detested the past and all that it held. I had spent so much time pushing the shame deeper and deeper within me that I had helped it grow and take control of everything about me. I had been no more rational with mine than Callie had been with hers.

I could see that the story touched Callie. Tears rolled down her face, but I could also see that my pain had not changed how she felt about herself. I wanted to fight for Callie and for myself. Callie rolled over and turned her back to me. I decided to leave her alone for now.

Darkness was setting in and I needed to attend to the women. They had become very efficient at helping themselves throughout the day. However, getting ready for bed was not easy for them or for me. For those who had left behind children, twilight reminded them of prayers and tucking their little ones in, of reading bedtime stories. We were all dealing with the unjustness of our situation and the darkness seemed to magnify it. At night pain echoed through the halls.

I started thinking of a poem I would put on paper before climbing into bed.

The Dark

At night the dark it holds me tight
And will not set me free
I fear the darkness with no light
For none are there for me

All hugs are hidden far away
No love is in my room
The darkness lingers as I lay
So full of fear and doom

No one to give their love to me
Or even say good-night
To let me know that I can flee
From darkness into light

Annie tapped me on the shoulder with a look of concern on her face.

"Annie, I am so worried and confused. I think long and hard about these women and what I can do for them."

"You do plenty for these women."

"Callie is slipping away. I see her dying a little more each and every day. I do not know what to do." I bowed my head in sadness.

"There's nothing more you can do. There's nothing any of us can do. She won't believe anything we tell her. She is so hard on herself. I think it is all truly driving her mad. Of all the women here, I think poor Callie has become the most indifferent to life. If we don't reach her soon, I fear she won't survive." Annie's tears rolled down her face and she looked as though it was taking all of her strength to hold back a sob. "A child carrying the burden of a woman."

"I agree. It is quite a helpless feeling to watch her slowly slip into despair." Grief caught in the back of my throat.

I could hardly wait to get back to my room. There were so many words that I longed to write down. They played like a sad song in my mind.

A Wall

She has built a wall
And built it tall
To keep us out
And keep her in
All but for another's sin

I had once thought death to be the worst thing that could happen. I now thought hopelessness was worse.

CHAPTER 33

I t had been a week since I told Callie my story and nothing had changed. Her shame, and her fear of the child inside her, held firm. Convinced that she would give birth to a monster, Callie had asked for it to be taken away as soon as it was born. Callie was not a cold-hearted woman but a badly broken child.

I would have to wait until the child was born before I could formulate a plan. What if she did bring a deformed baby into the world? I remembered the stories of how children born out of incest were disturbed and disfigured. As the months passed, the questions remained unanswered.

Talking Dr. Helsley into allowing the child to remain at Helsley House was not as hard as I had imagined, but only because taking the baby elsewhere might arouse questions. I was prepared to do all I could to help Callie and her baby. That is, if the baby could be loved.

As I helped the last woman into bed, I heard my name called.

"Isobel, Isobel. Come quickly." It was Callie.

When I reached her side, she whispered, "I have wet the bed. I am so sorry."

"Are you in pain?" I knew the answer already.

I had found a book in Dr. Helsley's library about childbirth and midwifery and read it from cover to cover more than once. I had only encountered childbirth one time in my life and that had not turned out well at all. I wanted to know what to expect when the baby came. I also wanted to keep an eye on Dr. Helsley and feel assured that he was doing everything he could to keep Callie and the baby safe.

"My back has been hurting all day." Tears coursed down Callie's face.

"Why did you not tell someone?"

"I just thought it was from my stomach growing larger."

The simplicity of a child, I thought. I tried to make Callie as comfortable as possible while summoning Dr. Helsley to come at once.

"You were correct in calling for me," the doctor said after performing a quick examination. "The baby is making its way into the world. It will not, however, be soon. There is nothing more I can do for her now." He huffed as he left the room.

Time crept by so slowly. I did not know who was more frightened, Callie or me. The best I could tell, it had been over twenty hours since Callie's water broke and I was not sure how much more she could withstand. Annie and I periodically checked on her as we attended to our other duties throughout the day.

As I was making my way back to check on Callie, I heard her pathetic cry. She was steadily growing weaker and I could see the excruciating pain on her face. I feared for both Callie's life and the baby's.

Callie's eyes pleaded. "I am dying, aren't I, Isobel? I am going to die. God is punishing me for what I did."

I called for Dr. Helsley to return and confirm my suspicion, for I was sure the birth was close at hand.

"No, you are not dying and you are not being punished. Listen to me and breathe," I said, in what I hoped was an unruffled tone.

Dr. Helsley examined Callie. "I can see the baby's head. It is coming. Now squeeze Isobel's hand and push," Dr. Helsley commanded Callie in what was a surprisingly soft tone. "Push, Callie. Push harder, push now," Dr. Helsley said louder but not in his usual harsh, condescending tone.

I had never seen my own mother's face, except for the pictures my grandmother showed me, but I was seeing her face now in place of Callie's.

I assured Callie, "You are not going to die," but I was not so sure.

After the third hard push and scream, the baby's head emerged. With the next push a girl was born. Dr. Helsley hastily handed the baby over to me and began attending to Callie.

The baby was so tiny I guessed her to weigh no more than a small sack of sugar, but she was lifeless and cold. Dread filled me.

"Do not die on me, little baby. You must live, do you hear me?"

No sooner had I spoken the words than she began to cry and flail her arms, my demand rewarded.

"Callie, do you hear that? Do you hear those lungs? She is beautiful. She is not a monster!" I cried.

As I turned toward Callie, my concern for her grew. The baby seemed to be in strong health, but Callie did not. Blood had begun to puddle between her legs. I had little faith in Dr. Helsley's medical expertise, but at the moment I had no choice but to trust him to help her.

"Move back, Isobel, I have to finish here. Take the baby and tend to her, now!" The apprehension in Dr. Helsley's voice caused my legs to move almost involuntarily to the other side of the small dark room.

CHAPTER 34

I took the baby back to my room and began cleaning her up in the washbasin. What little fingers and toes! One, two, three … there were ten of each. I looked her over closely and wrapped her in a small blanket that Annie had crocheted.

I took the baby back to show Callie just how beautiful she was, thankful that Dr. Helsley had indeed kept her alive.

"Isobel, don't leave me!" Callie whispered hoarsely.

"Be still, please. You do not need to move. The baby is not a monster at all. Look at her. She has all her toes and fingers, and what striking red hair. Why, it is the color of mine," I said, with a proud lilt in my voice, hoping to put Callie at ease. "She is absolutely beautiful, Callie, she is perfect."

"Do not speak of the baby. She is not perfect. You may have striking red hair, but so does my father. She is just like him. If she is beautiful on the outside, then she must be a monster on the inside. That's even worse. Get Annie to take her away, Isobel, please."

I had never heard her speak of her father's red hair. I had no idea that seeing the child would only make things worse.

Dr. Helsley suddenly returned to his former cold, harsh self. "She will be weak for a time, but she should survive this ordeal. Now see to the other women. Callie is not our only concern."

Annie unexpectedly appeared at my side, taking the baby from my arms.

"Go ahead, Isobel. I'll watch over Callie. As soon as she is able, this baby has to eat."

I had forgotten that. "Do you think you can get Callie to nurse her, Annie? As soon as I am finished with the women I will be back to help."

I returned shortly and could tell by Annie's face that she had not been successful.

"Callie won't let me put the baby near her. She pushes her away when I try."

I did not know what I would do if Callie refused to let the baby nurse. I spoke softly to her, begging her to feed the baby. Callie stared blankly at the ceiling as if I were not there. I picked up the baby and slowly eased her toward Callie, placing her next to Callie's breast. Callie did not resist.

"Look at her. She belongs to you as much as she does your father. Do not let him take that away from you."

Callie refused to look at the baby. I felt embarrassed as I manipulated Callie's breast into the baby's mouth, but I was not going to allow the wee thing to starve because of her mother's deteriorated mental state.

Later, I expressed my concerns on paper.

Just a Babe

With hair so red
And lungs so loud
You're all alone
Amongst a crowd

124

CHAPTER 35

I have allowed you to keep the baby close at hand for a week now in order to assure her health, but now I think it time we decide on her future. I have thought it over and decided an orphanage would be most appropriate."

I should have anticipated this reaction from Dr. Helsley, but his words still shocked me. "An orphanage?" I called out. My heart began to pound.

There was no way I would allow this child to be raised in an orphanage. I still hoped that Callie would come to her senses and fall in love with the baby as I already had. The baby did not belong to me, but I did not think I could have loved her any more. There was something quite different about her. I could not put my finger on it. She was, with no doubt, different, but not a monster.

"Miss McFadden, you have done quite well with the women, and I do not want anything upsetting that. You do not have time to do your job and coddle a baby. Something her mother certainly does not do," Dr. Helsley stated in a gruff, matter-of-fact tone.

"Please allow her to remain here, Dr. Helsley. I assure you she will not keep me from my duties. There is a constructive side to the baby's presence here, as well. She calms the women. The women miss being near their own children. It is as if they have adopted the baby as their own. Why, just yesterday Ella was having one of her crying episodes; and when I placed the baby in her lap, she at once settled down and began to sing."

I knew I was being selfish. Maybe the baby did need to go to an orphanage and be adopted by loving parents, but I could be a loving parent and I needed her.

Dr. Helsley had, in fact, noticed the women's response to the baby. He had mentioned more than once that he had never been around children much in his life but felt this child was unlike any he had encountered. Even he had noticed that she never cried and was quite content with any situation. I felt a kind of mother's pride when he spoke of her that way.

"Even if this were true, and it was possible to permit her to stay, do you think it better to raise a child in an insane asylum than an orphanage?" Dr. Helsley asked.

I knew for once in his life Dr. Helsley was speaking the truth. Had I not just thought the very same thoughts? It was selfish of me to refuse the child a better environment, but what if it was not better? What if she was never adopted? What if they were cruel to her? I loved this baby and refused to think anyone in the orphanage could love her as much. I had heard horrible stories of orphanages and almshouses.

I did not believe Dr. Helsley would do the right thing for the baby, whether or not he sent her to an orphanage. If he did, he would make sure he lost no money on the arrangement, which meant he would send her to a state run home, as a pauper. I could not bear the thought of it.

"I assure you, sir, I will manage. You will be most impressed by the situation, and it will be most beneficial to you. In keeping her here, no one will question the child's origin."

I knew Dr. Helsley wanted nothing about his practice to be questioned.

"I will give you one month and not a day more to show me how this situation will be of great benefit to me. If not, I will send her away. If she causes any problems or keeps you from doing your work, she will be gone immediately. Do you understand, Miss McFadden?"

"Most definitely, sir, it will work." I spoke the words with as much confidence as I could muster.

I held the baby with one hand and wrote with the other.

Mama's Lap

The coolness of a blowing breeze
The warmth of flowing sap
Both fill a child with life inside
Like Mama's loving lap

The winds that have no breeze at all
The trees that have no sap
Are like the empty child inside
Who's never felt that lap

So as you feel the gentle breeze
And feel the flowing sap
Think of all the children now
Who cry for Mama's lap

127

CHAPTER 36

After two weeks of begging Callie daily to name the baby, I decided I would give her a name myself. It was wrong to keep referring to her as "the baby."

"I am going to name you Kathryn Lynette and call you Katy. Kathryn was my mother's name, and Lynette is Callie's mother's name." Katy smiled and cooed and nuzzled her cheek against mine as if to tell me she liked my choice of names.

Katy reminded me of myself. She was no more a monster than I was a witch. In fact, Katy was quite the opposite. She looked like a little angel, her face clear and unblemished, her cheeks pink and rosy and her hair such a brilliant shade of red. It was her eyes, however, that continually caught my attention. They were dark and lucid. There was no distinction between the center of her eye and the color surrounding it. They were totally black and so alert.

I glanced over and noticed Callie watching us. She and I had barely carried on a conversation since Katy's birth. Her strength had been steadily improving, but her mind had not.

She wanted no more to do with Katy now than she had the day she was born.

"Callie, will you not give Katy a chance? She is such a good baby, so loving. I have named her Kathryn Lynnette, after both our mothers."

Callie continued looking past me with that distant stare I would never become accustomed to. She then leaned forward and whispered in my direction. "Leave it be, Isobel. She is a monster, whether you see it or not. I will have nothing to do with her. There is more to the eye than you can see. You are blinded by love."

I felt such sorrow for her. It seemed she was willing herself to believe that Katy was evil, as if the only way she could cope was by refusing to fall in love with a child that she felt revealed the sins of her past. I decided it would be the last time I pleaded for Callie to love her daughter.

It was then that Callie leaned forward once more and whispered, "Isobel, I fear that life is not as it shows itself to be. When doors close, evil appears. When a mother bears a child she cannot stand to look at and a father is so filled with evil, then the child must be born unto itself, becoming in itself what is needed to survive. It is better to be born unto oneself, than to be born unto evil, for evil can surely only breed more evil."

Her words sounded as though they belonged to someone else, someone much older with a deep personal knowledge of wickedness. I looked at Katy and tried to forget what Callie had said, but the chill coursing through my veins would not.

I had to dwell on the care of the child now, and pray that Callie's mind would clear; as my poems helped my mind to clear.

Katy

With eyes so black and hair so red
A smile so big and bright
Little one with lies unsaid
For you the world's not right

No father's hugs to chase the fears
Or kisses for your pain
No mother's love to wipe the tears
Or guard you from the rain

You do not know that's not the way
The world was meant to be
A child who's born and made to pay
For love that should be free

How different it will be for you
For I will always care
The smile you show will be brand new
For this smile we will share

CHAPTER 37

I f not for the help from Lonzo and Annie and Katy's easy temperament, I could not have done it. Somehow, together we made it work. My job at Helsley House was not suffering, and Katy was being well cared for, a true blessing. If Lonzo and Annie were busy when I needed to be away from Katy, she would lie in the crib that Lonzo made and play or nap. She never cried. She was such a happy and contented baby.

"Miss McFadden, could you please assist me in the treatment room?" Dr. Helsley asked one afternoon. It was the request I dreaded most of all.

Not this madness again. It happened two, sometimes three times a week. My fear that Dr. Helsley would use his harsh, abusive tactics on Callie had not come to be. Even he could surely see that it would be a futile attempt.

"Katy, you be quiet for your mother now." I had come to think of Katy as my own, even calling myself her mother. I could not bear for the child to have no one to belong to.

It seemed a bit soon for Dr. Helsley to request my assistance. He had just yesterday ordered Bessie downstairs to the treatment room for what he called "medical breakthroughs." Bessie was a loud and boisterous woman who could find humor in most anything. She did a fairly good job of holding her own with Dr. Helsley. Nonetheless, she feared the treatment room no less than the others. She referred to it as "the sinister doctor's fun house."

Bessie had been sent to Helsley House with a diagnosis of neurasthenia due to complaints of headaches and fatigue. She was wealthy, and by what I gathered, some of her family did not agree with how she chose to spend her money. By having her declared insane, they could take control of all her assets.

"Do come now, Miss McFadden, we have much work to do."

Rarely did Dr. Helsley conduct his experiments two days in a row.

This time it was Lucy who was taken downstairs to the treatment room. She had become hysterical, screaming for her son. Dr. Helsley relied on my calming Lucy to make it easier for him to maneuver her into the treatment room. If there was one thing Dr. Helsley did not like, it was opposition.

If not for these maddening experiments, I would not have thought this the worst place in the world. Dr. Helsley took pride in running an asylum for "the upper class women," as he liked to call them. At least here the women roomed together in groups and had cots on which to sleep. Nonetheless, the experiments in the treatment room were barbaric. I doubted the family members or inspectors who showed up periodically ever saw this part of the asylum.

Lucy had left behind a five-month-old baby at her home in Ohio. Her husband had misled her into believing he was bringing her to a woman's boarding house for a few days to recuperate from her weakened state after childbirth. When Lucy found out that he betrayed her, she was heartbroken.

"Quiet now, Lucy. The sooner we begin, the sooner we can finish," Dr. Helsley said with an annoyed look on his face.

Lucy repeated the same words each time Dr. Helsley came near her. "I am not weak of mind or insane. I merely became tired and weak from caring for a child who had colic and rarely slept. If I had family or a husband to help me at night with my son, I would have gotten rest and my strength back. I am not demented!" she cried out accusingly, as she always did.

I begged Lucy to calm down, with promises of her seeing Katy when the ordeal was over. My words helped. She wept, but no longer screamed out or fought. She missed her child. All she needed was to have him placed in her arms, not some brutal experiment that Dr. Helsley would use to miraculously heal her.

"Isobel, do hurry, we do not have all day," Dr. Helsley ordered, growing more irritable with each second of delay.

Lucy's diagnosis of neurosis was never treated the same way twice. This time he strapped her to a metal bed and injected a clear liquid into her arm. I did not ask what it was and he did not offer any explanation. It made Lucy's body convulse and she wet on herself. Dr. Helsley handed me a cloth to place in her mouth as her body thrashed about.

It was nearly two hours before Lucy was strong enough to be helped from the table. I took her back to the ward, cleaned her, and helped her into bed. I then checked on Katy. She was not in our room, but I knew where to find her. Annie loved to take the baby to the kitchen and fix her bottle at mealtime. Katy was now drinking milk from a cow. Callie's health and apathy had made it impossible for her to continue to nurse.

Dr. Helsley had changed Annie's title from kitchen help to matron attendant and to our surprise, hired Martha Brewer to work in the kitchen, but no one could cook like Annie. Her knowledge of herbs and spices and good home cooking could not be surpassed. We were all happy that Annie still dabbled in the kitchen.

I do not know why Dr. Helsley hired someone else, other than that it being difficult for me to assist him in the basement and care for the women at the same time.

Martha was a gruff woman, lacking both the warmth and the empathy that Annie possessed. I was glad Dr. Helsley placed her in the kitchen and not with me, even if it meant sacrificing a few good meals. Hopefully, Annie could teach her a thing or two about cooking. I was certain it would be easier than teaching her compassion.

CHAPTER 38

Though I had told Callie I had accepted my father's words as that of a heartbroken drunkard, I could not put them totally to rest. I had been thinking about my life more and more lately, dwelling on questions revisited over a thousand times. What if my mother had not died? What if my father had thought of me as his daughter and not a witch who could take the form of any creature? What if, what if, what if? I wished the words *what if* did not exist. They did nothing but make me think about things that could not be changed.

If I had felt loved and trusted instead of shamed and disgraced, would I have still become the same person? Maybe I would be worse off. What a strange thought.

It was time for me to accept my life and stop dreaming. I had already dreamed my childhood away. I would write one more poem dwelling upon my childhood and then I would put it away. I had to before it took my mind as Callie's had been taken.

Hatred

Why was I born into that place
So full of dark and gloom
Where love and beauty had no face
For hatred filled the room

He looked at me who killed his wife
So filled with grief and pain
For I had come into his life
And there I would remain

The strength he had I did not hold
To see the world with hate
For when I looked I saw no cold
But warmth that could not wait

He had no faith in life at all
To God he did not speak
For him the earth was but a ball
The Lord some kind of freak

I feel ashamed that I must hide
To show emotions here
But as I grow I know inside
To love is what I fear

I must learn to stop the pity and start the fight, not only for myself, but for Katy. I wanted her to grow up happy and content with who she was. I wanted her to know that she was loved and accepted for just being Katy.

CHAPTER 39

Two years had passed since Katy's birth, with no more discussions of sending her away. She was intelligent beyond her age and more than a blessing to all the women. Callie, on the other hand, had nothing to do with Katy, and our relationship suffered because of it.

"She is one smart little girl. Look at the beautiful picture Katy drew," Annie said, while holding out the drawing for me to inspect.

I turned the paper around to the right and then back to the left. Annie and I burst out laughing. "It's a tree," Annie explained.

She and Lonzo took such pride in Katy. When I was not trying to teach Katy something new, they were. I had pleaded with Dr. Helsley to order Katy a few picture books. He had agreed and deducted the purchases from my wages. Dr. Helsley paid me in cash, which I kept it hidden in a tin box under a loose floorboard in my room. What did I need money for? I had not left the asylum in over six years.

"It's hard to believe that Katy already knows her colors and how to count to ten." Annie said.

Before I could agree, I heard a boisterous laugh coming from the hallway. "Go ahead, Isobel," Martha Brewer said to me. "I'll help Annie. You tend to Corrine."

When Martha first arrived, she had been insistent on following Dr. Helsley's rules and responding only to him. She refused to call us by our first names and was slow to carry on idle conversation.

I had not thought it possible, but Martha Brewer became a friend. She was by no means like Norna or Annie, but she cast a smile my way and listened when I needed an ear. She remained gruff, but not unkind. I took that to be just her way.

"Miss McFadden, are you in the kitchen?" Dr. Helsley called. No matter how many times I assisted Dr. Helsley, I never grew accustomed to the sick feeling in my stomach whenever he called for my help.

I knew that whatever Dr. Helsley was going to do would only aggravate the problem. Corinne Bryant had a nervous temperament and laughed incessantly when worry threatened to overtake her. Dr. Helsley was sure the extreme bouts of laughter were due to fits of hysteria. He considered it a strong sign of insanity.

I accompanied Dr. Helsley and Corinne to the treatment room. On the way down the stairs, Dr. Helsley began explaining his thoughts and continued with the procedures he would be doing. I could not understand why he insisted on telling me. He knew how much I hated that. A nurse should have been assisting him, but then no real nurse would stand for his methods. Although, I had read only this morning in the newspaper of a nurse who had been dismissed from her duties for slapping and pulling the hair of a woman who refused to take her medicine. The supervisor who dismissed her was surely a more kindly man than Dr. Helsley.

Dr. Helsley proceeded with his explanation of the situation. "Corinne becomes agitated and laughs uncontrollably on the slightest provocation. Therefore, I must look for alternative methods in curing her. The intense excitability she displays during her menses leads me to believe her problem is due to the excitability of her uterus. Thus, she will receive a series of hot water cleanses through a tubing placed inside her and directed toward her uterus. This should calm her unbalanced uterine system. We will begin with the first cleansing today."

I could not bring myself to look Corinne in the eyes for fear of what I would see. I held her hand and turned my head as Dr. Helsley began the procedure. I felt the guilt of being a coward for allowing these atrocities to continue. But if doctors signed statements declaring these women insane, then what Dr. Helsley did was completely legal—wrong, but legal.

I had read that some doctors used a procedure called psycho-analysis when dealing with the insane. Reports described it as more humane and offering more hope. But what did I know of the real ways of the world? My only knowledge of the world came from what I read. What if the real world was even worse than Helsley House?

No sooner was Dr. Helsley finished and gone than Annie appeared at my side. "Isobel, I'll help Corinne back to her room while you go check on Katy." Annie was such a blessing. It was late, and yet she was kind enough to relieve me of my duties in the treatment room, knowing that I had spent little time lately with Katy.

Many times either Annie or Lonzo assisted me in getting the patient back to her room. Dr. Helsley was drinking more and more. I had heard him on several occasions talking to himself in his room after retiring for the night.

We were overworked, but I do not think any of us minded. We worked well together and we cared about the women. We also shared a fear of someone finding out about Katy. None of us wanted to risk her being taken away.

As I slipped quietly back in my room, I watched as Katy lay silently across the bed looking at a picture book. Was it normal for a two-year-old to sit so still? I was not sure.

CHAPTER 40

The months turned into years and Callie continued living in a state of malaise, seeming to have given up on life itself. Though I repeatedly assured her of Katy's intelligence and beauty, Callie kept insisting that it was nothing but lies and the truth would kill us all.

I often thought of Callie's parents and how they could allow their daughter to remain in such a place. I could understand Callie's father not wanting the truth known, but what of Callie's mother? Was Callie correct in believing that her mother knew nothing of her whereabouts? What would Callie's mother think of Katy? No matter how many times I promised myself that I would not talk to Callie about Katy, I broke that promise. My words would not penetrate the wall that she had built.

It was time to stop trying for something that was not to be. I felt as if I were pushed against a wall that Callie had built and so that is what I wrote.

The Wall

She built a wall so high and strong
I almost made it fall
But once again she built it back
Without a door and tall

She put in windows shaded dark
Where no one could see in
But looking out to see the world
She saw it all as sin

All the women looked away
And passed her right on by
Her heart and soul were out of reach
Behind the wall she'd die

Katy grew stronger and healthier with each passing year. She entertained the women by singing, dancing, and reading them stories. Learning to read came easily to her.

She had just finished reading one of her new primer books when she leaped off the bed and asked, "Mama, where is Lonzo?"

"He has gone to take Mrs. Brewer to the train station. He will not return until tomorrow. Is there anything I can do to help?"

"He said I could help him plant some flowers."

"Well, I am sure *he* has not forgotten. As soon as he returns, you and Lonzo will be able to plant flowers. Now go play."

I tried to hide my sadness over Martha Brewer's departure. She had fallen on the outside steps while pouring out a dishpan of water. Dr. Helsley had asked Lonzo to take her to the train station where she was to meet someone. Unable to walk, Martha was no use in the kitchen. Annie and I would feel her loss; she had become quite helpful to us. She had not however, become empathetic toward the women. She remained in the kitchen and rarely if ever conversed with them, fearing their so-called madness.

Dr. Helsley announced that no one would be hired to replace Mrs. Brewer. It was just as well.

By Katy's fifth birthday, she already spoke and behaved as a child twice her age. A day never passed that she did not surprise me with her intelligence. If Callie would have allowed herself, she could have been quite proud of her daughter. Instead, I was proud of *my* daughter.

Callie took up more of my thoughts than I liked. I felt so helpless. In worrying about her I thought of yet another poem.

A Tomb

She slinks down in her lonely chair
And looks across the room
I see a soul whose face is gone
A guard of her own tomb

In youth, I see her so alive
Her warmth now turned so cold
The worst part of the tomb itself
There's no one there to hold

CHAPTER 41

As I finished gulping down a cup of hot tea that had nearly scalded my tongue, Katy came running toward me and hid behind my skirt. Katy rarely showed such emotion, especially fear.

"Katy, for heaven's sake, what is wrong? Tell me what makes you behave in such a manner."

"I did not do anything wrong. I was just talking to Amelia, when Dr. Helsley scolded me. I smiled and wished him a good morning. Do you know what he said then?"

"No, but I am sure you will tell me."

"He said that children were a menace to society. He said, 'Children should neither be seen nor heard. Little snotty-nosed children are a disgrace and should be muzzled and chained.'"

"Oh, Katy, surely you must be mistaken." Dr. Helsley could be very cruel, but I had never seen him direct his cruelty toward Katy.

"He did Mama, I promise." Katy said with her eyes opened wide.

I did not understand Dr. Helsley's verbal attack. Katy was never loud or rude and certainly not a so-called snotty-nosed child.

"Katy, run on and get dressed for bed while I finish helping Amelia. I will be up shortly."

Whatever could have possessed Dr. Helsley to say that to Katy? I was sure he had spoken the words; Katy would not make up such a thing. But I knew also I would not question him about it. I would not say anything to bring unwanted attention to Katy. I returned to our room and found Katy twirling a tuft of hair along with Callie's hair ribbon around her finger, the only thing of her mother's she owned. I had kept it in my bureau until Katy found it.

"Mama, look, isn't it beautiful? May I wear it?"

"Only if you promise to take very good care of it can you keep it. That ribbon belonged to someone very special."

"I promise, Mama. I will be very careful."

I felt it right for Katy to have the hair ribbon—a piece of her mother—her real mother.

From then on Katy kept it with her always. I knew she loved it because it was pretty, and not for any other reason.

CHAPTER 42

I pulled the hair ribbon out of Katy's hair and placed in on the bureau before I began the nightly routine of brushing her hair. As Katy sat quietly, I thought back to the day I had taken the ribbon.

"Callie, I must take the ribbon from your hair. You will not be allowed to keep it."

"Please, no," the small, scared girl had cried. "I have worn it in my hair since the day my mother made it for me. It is the only thing I have from home."

The ribbon was a delicate pink, edged in lace. "My mother made it for me on my thirteenth birthday. I want my mother. Please help me to get home. Please."

I had turned away to keep Callie from seeing my tears or the hopelessness of her situation. She would surely see home no sooner than I would.

I slipped the ribbon inside Callie's pocket and made her promise to keep it hidden, or she and I would both suffer the cost. For the moment, it was enough to calm Callie.

It was later, as her mental state declined, that I took it back to my room.

"Mama, it's time for bed." Katy's voice brought me back to the present.

"And so it is, my little princess."

"I'm ready for my story," Katy said with the same anticipation as the first time she heard it.

"Well, hop into bed."

"Mama, tell me again the story of the ribbon." Katy smiled up at me.

Katy's favorite bedtime story was one that I had invented about the ribbon. As I tucked Katy into bed, I began the bedtime story we called, "The Story of the Magic Ribbon."

"Once upon a time there was a beautiful girl named Katy," I began.

"Just like me; right, Mama?"

I nodded and continued with the story. "She lived in a castle filled with servants and a mother who loved her more than anything in the whole world.

"There was something very special about Katy; she owned a magical ribbon. Each section of lace on the ribbon held a wish inside. Katy knew that whatever bad happened to her would pass because Katy only had to wish upon the ribbon to make it better. Katy also knew she could not waste her wishes, just in case things ever got really, really bad. Katy clung to her ribbon and saved her wishes."

That was as far as my story progressed before Katy's eyes closed and sleep took over.

I hoped Katy would understand the hidden meaning of my story, that no matter how hopeless life might seem, each problem would surely pass and with time things would be better. I never wanted her to think that things were at their absolute worst, because no matter what, circumstances can always get worse. I knew that almost seemed brutal to teach a small child, but I wanted to prepare her for the harshness of life, and to never underestimate the power of evil.

Katy lived in an insane asylum with two mothers, one who Katy truly belonged to but who could not love her, and one Katy did not belong to but who truly loved her. Somewhere far away she had a father who was also her grandfather. With that kind of life, things, indeed, could always get worse.

CHAPTER 43

I t had been a cold and harsh winter. The only consolation was that it gave Dr. Helsley little time to focus on Katy. From time to time she mentioned that Dr. Helsley spoke harshly to her. I was confounded as to why he spoke such unkind words when Katy went out of her way to be polite and kind to him. It broke my heart to watch her seek out his kindness. I had come to the conclusion that Dr. Helsley was not always in his right mind. I was grateful for Lonzo, who presented himself as a father figure to her.

The coldness of winter had brought with it a sickness that was running rampant. Two women had died in the last week and more were becoming ill. But no amount of hardship had prepared us for what was yet to come.

The ground was frozen solid, which made it extremely difficult for Lonzo to dig the graves. Lonzo also had to declare the last woman, Patricia, dead when she passed away. Dr. Helsley said he was feeling ill and that Lonzo knew what death looked like as well as he did. That was so unlike Dr. Helsley, who took his position as a doctor to be almost god-like. Dr. Helsley only signed the certificate. He never saw the face of death on Patricia.

I had grown accustomed to preparing bodies for burial. My only solace for the latest deaths was that the women were both of such an advanced age. It was by no means easier to see them die or to lose those I had come to love, but believing them to have led a long life brought solace.

I continued my writing, not only for my own sanity, but in hopes that someday it could be of value to someone, to anyone. Norna had taught me much about the power in pen and paper. Sometimes it was the only way I could free myself of unwanted feelings. Silence had become my tormenter. There were things that happened at Helsley House that the world should know about. The world needed to hear these women's stories. As I looked around at their faces, I could see that these poor souls were no different from anyone else. Nobody could understand what made them do the things they did. But I understood. I understood only too well what made them cry out in the night or scratch themselves until they bled. It was neither madness nor insanity.

My mind drifted constantly back to Norna. I had been reading everything I could about the suffrage movement. In the last paper I read Carrie Chapman Catt had succeeded Susan B. Anthony as president of the National American Woman Suffrage Association, who was stepping down to care for her ailing husband.

I had read many articles that had been written by Susan B. Anthony. She, along with Elizabeth Cady Stanton, had started a newspaper, *The Revolution*. I was sure she must be one of Norna's favorite writers. Mrs. Anthony fought relentlessly for women's rights. She had even persuaded the University of Rochester to admit women. How I hoped one day Katy could attend college.

Mrs. Anthony had also been a strong advocate for the slaves and worked with a man named Frederick Douglass to fight for abolition. That would make her one of Annie's favorites, also. Annie was a lot like Norna in wanting equality for all people. It made me laugh to imagine those two together. The world would never be the same.

Once after Annie and I had talked about Norna, and I explained her fiery spirit and her fight for women's rights, Annie took out a piece of paper from her Bible and read a quotation from Sojourner Truth to me: "If the first woman God ever made was strong enough to turn the world upside down all alone, these women together ought to be able to turn it back and get it right side up again." Annie explained that Sojourner Truth was a black woman who fought for Negroes' rights and women's rights. One day I prayed Norna and Annie could meet.

Dr. Helsley's library had certainly filled my mind with knowledge. I might not know as much as Norna or Annie, but I was certainly on my way. I had wanted to find a bountiful number of books in America, and did just that. As Annie said, "There is good in all things." In this dark place, I had found good things in spite of the misery.

I read articles that had been written by other suffragettes that I was sure Norna had read as well: Lucy Stone, Julia Ward Howe, and Lucretia Mott, to name a few. I also found a copy of *Woman, Church and State* written by Matilda Joslyn Gage, that was most interesting. I was not sure why Dr. Helsley had a copy of it. Perhaps he wanted to know what women were accomplishing in the world and what he had to fear. I copied quotes and articles to keep in my room. I would have cut them out and kept them close to my heart if I had not been afraid Dr. Helsley would notice them missing.

I wished Callie could talk with me about the great things women were doing. Callie, Norna, Annie and I could have had a grand time together discussing the injustices of the world.

I had hoped that by now Callie would have improved, but nothing had changed. I feared she was lost to the world, and recorded my concerns.

Why

Why should she bare her soul
For pain
Letting others see her
Shame

Telling thoughts no one
Should know
Shedding tears that
Should not flow

Opening eyes for all
To see
Expectations that
Cannot be

CHAPTER 44

I continued to miss my friendship with Callie and was becoming exceedingly worried. In her constant state of sadness and hopelessness, her health had declined; her body a weakened vessel. Though she rarely spoke a word, she was now complaining of abdominal pains. I prayed it was not cholera, the name Dr. Helsley had given the current illness plaguing us.

I had read about cholera and found it to be a sickness as awful as described. Dr. Helsley never explained why it had infected Helsley House. I thought it may have come through our most recent woman. She had been the first to get sick. Others claimed it was contamination from unclean sources. I dwelled less on how it came to be than how and when it would end.

"Come quickly, Isobel. It's Callie," Annie whispered in my ear so as not to upset Katy. The truth was, I believed Katy would be no more upset than if it were any other woman in the asylum. Why should she be? She knew nothing about her parentage and Callie had never shown the faintest interest in her.

I cringed when I reached Callie's room. She was lying on the floor soaked in her own waste, holding her stomach and moaning in pain. My prayer had not been answered. I could see by the sweat on her brow and the look in her eyes that Callie was consumed with cholera.

"Get Dr. Helsley at once. Hurry, Annie!"

Several minutes passed before Annie returned with Dr. Helsley, whom she found walking the grounds. He had taken to spending more time in his room or outside since this dreadful disease came to Helsley House. I think he feared exposure.

He only had to look at Callie briefly. "You were correct in your worries. She has cholera and it is beyond anything medicine can heal. Due to her weakened state, I fear it has advanced quickly. I will administer small doses of opium and camphor and we shall hope for a large miracle."

I was sure Callie would die. Miracles had never come to this girl's aid. How unfair life was! At only nineteen—she was still a child herself. What would Callie's mother feel if she knew her child was dying? Her father would surely feel nothing more than delight.

Dr. Helsley quickly took command in a tone that was filled with a concern I had not heard from him since Katy's birth.

"Lonzo, clean the floor immediately. We must stop this God-forsaken disease from spreading anymore. Annie, clean Callie up and help her to bed."

I began to tremble, knowing without a doubt that we had a reason to be troubled.

"Yes, Dr. Helsley." Annie said with alarm.

"She has little time left." I sensed he understood the situation was an uneasy one for me to bear.

In bed I stared at the ceiling and feared my mind was giving in to it all. I reached over and picked up my pen. It was time to write.

The Pathway of My Mind

My head is pounding
With such force
Its path's a maze
There is no course

There is no single
Lane ahead
But many trails
Are there instead

As sad as I felt, facing Callie's death was not as hard as I expected, for I had lost her the moment Katy entered the world. My mother's life had been lost as I took my first breath; Callie's mind had been lost the moment Katy had taken her first breath.

As Callie passed on in the early morning hours, it was Lonzo who once again viewed the body and relayed the news to Dr. Helsley.

Dr. Helsley continued to sign the death certificates as if nothing had changed. He was beginning to face his own demise and could not look death in the face as easily as he did once upon a time. I felt the doctor no longer embraced death as merely a part of life.

CHAPTER 45

Katy had been counting down the days until Christmas. It was Katy's sixth Christmas with us. How could time pass so quickly? Because of Katy, time seemed to have no limits. Her contagious laughter brought joy wherever she went.

Katy was in the cellar with Lonzo getting potatoes for dinner. Tonight she was going to help Annie prepare her famous Christmas Eve meal of baked ham, potato rissole, mulled cider, and huckleberry scones. The scones were a favorite of mine and had come from my own recipe. It was the only holiday of the year that Dr. Helsley relented and allowed Annie to prepare a special meal.

The only other time of year we had such a feast was when the Lunacy Board came to inspect Helsley House. At first I was amazed at how Dr. Helsley managed to pass an inspection with such high marks. Later Lonzo explained the doctor's tactics. He was very wealthy, and that meant more to the Lunacy Board than the women did. So he went out of his way to impress the board. That distressed me deeply.

After dinner, Katy followed me on my routine, helping the women get dressed for bed. She laid their bedclothes out as

I made sure each changed into them. It could have been an awkward feat for a child, but not for Katy.

In the last room we checked for the night, Katy reached into my pocket and found a tiny mirror. Dr. Helsley did not allow mirrors in the asylum for fear the women would cut themselves. I believed it was also part of their punishment for being women. Vanity was considered a female flaw. I had come into possession of the mirror when I found it in the belongings of a new patient named Ruby earlier in the day, glad I discovered it instead of Dr. Helsley. I had missed it when I went through her belongings earlier in the week. Ruby came to Helsley House because of a deep depression that seemed only natural to me. Her mother, brother, sister, and small daughter had drowned in a flood. How could someone survive that much tragedy?

As Katy looked into the mirror, she stared at her reflection and twisted her nose in a peculiar fashion.

"Don't play with your nose, Katy," Laura, who had been committed for being feeble-minded said as I was helping her with her bedclothes. "You know you'll turn into a monster if you do."

"Mama, can little girls really turn into monsters?" Katy asked.

"Of course not, you know that is silly. I told you not to believe everything the women say. Remember how I told you that they get confused sometimes?" I said it through clenched teeth so no one would overhear. I disliked that the women repeated stories of monsters to Katy, but poor Laura mimicked those around her and often did not understand the meaning of her words.

The women had heard Callie crying out that Katy would become a monster. I had tried to explain that those fears were nothing more than the ravings of a young mother driven to believe such a thing.

Katy once again looked into the mirror. She swore the eyes in the mirror did not belong to her.

"There's another girl looking back at me," she insisted. Her words frightened me, but I dismissed them as child's play.

That evening I opened my bureau drawer and wrote a new poem. As I read it back I found the words were distressing.

Mirror

Mirror, mirror in my hand
Those two eyes I see
Belong to someone I don't know
They do not come from me

There is another one I fear
Who dwells inside my soul
Who shares the vision in my eyes
To make my body whole

I wrote this as if looking through Katy's eyes, though Katy could have written it herself. She had followed in my footsteps and started writing poetry. Her poetry was exceptionally good for a child her age. I was forever finding new poems Katy had written.

I wanted nothing more than to dismiss what Katy said as purely a game of pretend, such as I had played many times as a child. Katy had been speaking more and more in an odd fashion. It was unlikely, yet I found myself fearing that maybe Callie had been right and there was more to Katy than the rest of us could see. How silly. Katy was just a little girl, a beautiful little girl, and no more.

The stress of Callie's passing weighed heavily on my mind. Or maybe Helsley House was finally consuming me.

It was then another poem came to me, this one from my fears. Had I taken away Katy's only possibility of living a normal life?

Children

Little children never seen
Come and play with me
Let me know I'm not alone
Please come and let me see

Let me see the games you play
The way you laugh and shout
Take me from this darkened place
Please help me to get out

I've never laughed and played at all
But heard the way you do
Come and show me how it's done
Please let me play with you

What had been done was done. It was of no use worrying about now. Worry and guilt would surely be the death of me.

I asked Katy to fetch me some clean sheets. After more than ten minutes had passed, I began to worry; Katy had not returned, which was quite unlike her. She was most punctual, especially for a child.

Suddenly, Annie came running toward me, shouting something about Katy. My heart sank.

"It's Katy! She's crying that her stomach hurts and you know she doesn't complain."

"Take care of the women, Annie."

All I could think of was cholera. Surely it had not returned. It had been over two weeks since anyone became sick. I had made sure to keep Katy away from the women who had become ill. She spent most of her time in our room during that time, or with Lonzo in the cottage.

As I entered the cottage, I could see that he was holding Katy out for Dr. Helsley to examine. It was with this blow I feared I would lose any of my remaining sanity. *God, please do not take Katy, too.* I hoped it was a case of indigestion and nothing more. My mind had ceased to think rationally.

Katy lay small and colorless in Lonzo's vast arms. She began to wail and thrash her arms about. I could barely stand to watch.

"I am afraid it is cholera," Dr. Helsley said, almost under his breath. He had made this diagnosis from a distance, barely looking across the room at Katy. He feared infection from this all-encompassing sickness so much so he was taking no chances.

"How can that be?" I wanted to scream. "It has been weeks since the last outbreak."

Dr. Helsley did not answer. Instead, he made swift preparations to isolate Katy from the women. It was Lonzo's quick thinking that came to the rescue.

"Katy can stay here in my quarters and Annie can help me watch over her. We can't put her around the others and start the outbreak all over again."

Lonzo had worked for Dr. Helsley for many years and made it through countless epidemics. He was, without a doubt, a strong man. I thanked God again for his swift thinking. We both knew that Dr. Helsley would not approve of my staying at Katy's bedside to nurse her. Dr. Helsley would not want any routine at the asylum disturbed.

"Thank you, Lonzo," I whispered.

"Do we still have plenty of sulphate of zinc?" Dr. Helsley asked, then turned and nearly ran from the room before receiving an answer.

Katy could not die. I could not bear the thought of being alone in this world, not again. As much as I called the women my own, it was Katy who meant everything to me.

"Do not look so sad, Mama. I am not very sick, really. Don't cry, please. My stomach really does not hurt much." As Katy's words escaped her lips so did the tears from my eyes.

I swore to myself that if Katy did not die, I would do anything within my power to make her life better. I was not sure there was a God, but I would not miss this one chance to pray for him to heal Katy. I prayed with all my power. "God, if Katy lives, I promise you I will fight a battle unlike anyone has fought before. I will make it right for her."

CHAPTER 46

I t had been a restless night. I wanted nothing more than to be lying next to Katy. I wanted to check on her but first I had to help the women with breakfast. I could not risk upsetting Dr. Helsley. This was not how I had envisioned spending Christmas morning. It was then I noticed him out of the corner of my eye, rushing toward me.

"You must come to my office at once, Isobel. Annie will take care of the women."

Something was wrong. Annie often assisted me, but rarely replaced me. As I searched Annie's face for answers, Annie avoided my eyes. I pleaded for a look to ease my thoughts. I found none.

"Isobel, please shut the door behind you, and have a seat." Dr. Helsley said as he handed me a glass of water.

"Just tell me what you have to say, Dr. Helsley. You are frightening me."

"Katy worsened during the night and there was nothing more any of us could do."

"What was he saying? What did he mean about nothing more to be done? What mean trick was he playing now?"

I knew what he was trying to tell me, but I could not believe it to be the truth. I was close to hysterics. "She did not die. You are wrong! I have scrubbed and cleaned everything. I have kept her away from the women."

"No it is you that is wrong. Katy succumbed to the cholera sometime in the night. Lonzo said that she was not in pain. She is gone, Isobel. I am sorry. Lonzo has taken care of the necessary precautions."

What a coward. Once again Lonzo had to do his job. *I do not think it is death that Dr. Helsley fears so, but Hell itself.*

I could not think, nor breathe, nor hear. I felt the room begin to spin. Dr. Helsley's lips were moving, but no sound was coming out of his mouth. The silence was deafening.

A poem. I needed a poem to ward off the hysteria I felt close at hand.

The Silence

From in this cold there's no escape
I'm held a prisoner tight
Her arms of love are gone from me
Her warmth fled in the night

Katy had nothing more than a stomach ache. I was sure of it. Otherwise I would never have left her, not even for one night. No one dies a painless death from cholera. He was lying. I wanted it to be a lie. I wanted anything but this. Katy could not be dead, not the only person who had ever truly loved me. The only person I ever loved so profoundly. *God help me.* I could not go on. I did not want to go on. I wanted to be with Katy. I had no more life left in me than Callie had in her.

All I could see was Katy's face. I had caused Katy's death, as surely as if I had given her cholera myself. I had been selfish with her.

How could I ever live with myself? Guilt far worse than any I had experienced would surely follow me now for the rest of my life.

CHAPTER 47

I woke with my head pounding. I sat up and looked around. Where was Katy? It was then I remembered. Dr. Helsley must have given me something in my drink to make me sleep. I tried to clear my mind. I had to get moving. I looked around my room and the absence of Katy was more than I could stand. I needed to see her, but first I had something to do.

I knocked loudly on Dr. Helsley's office door and burst in before being requested. "Dr. Helsley, never make the mistake of drugging me again." Anger and pain had removed my inhibitions.

"It was only for your benefit that I did so," Dr. Helsley answered. "Before you say anything more I would like to say that I am sorry for the child's death. I will ask Annie to prepare Katy for burial. I know how hard this is, and I would not ask such a thing of you. Whatever you think, I am not that cruel."

"That is quite all right. I will do what needs to be done," I answered, with tears rolling down my cheeks and a feeling of anguish I had never known.

I refused to allow Dr. Helsley to escort me out to Lonzo's. I needed to be alone in my misery. I needed to get my wits about me.

I entered Lonzo's small, cozy quarters and immediately felt the warmth that Helsley House lacked. I saw Lonzo standing by the fire and my heart went out to him. I knew he loved Katy almost as much as I did.

"How did this happen, Lonzo? I did not even realize she was that sick. She had not eaten much lately but I thought she only had an upset stomach. How could she have gotten so sick so quickly? She was so strong. Not weak like the others."

"You know Katy. She never complains." Lonzo said.

I could not bear looking into Lonzo's suffering eyes. I could see that he needed to say something. Lonzo took so much responsibility upon himself.

"Lonzo, you must not blame yourself for her death. It was my fault. I should have known. I am her mother, or at least the only mother she has known. I allowed her to act older than her actual years. I should have made her be the little girl she was. I should not have let her behave like an adult in the body of a child. She should not have felt the need to hide her sickness. I am sure it was to protect me."

"Now, Isobel stop torturing yourself. I am not blaming myself for Katy's death, just for allowing you and her to have stayed here for so long. I should have made you take her and yourself away a long time ago. This is no place for either of you. There is a whole world out there and neither of you have gotten to see a minute of it. Now have a seat, Isobel. There's more to this than you know. I have to show you something. Please, sit down."

As I turned to sit, immediately my mouth flew open and my heart began to race. Once again I thought my mind had given in to the madness of this place.

"Is this another of my fanciful dreams? Have I delved so deeply into my imagination that I no longer know the difference from what is real?" I stared at the ghost in front of me.

"No, this is not a dream. It is your daughter. She is alive." Lonzo's face immediately changed from dark and grave to bright and hopeful.

Katy's striking black eyes looked into mine. I heard the most beautiful sound imaginable.

"Mama, Mama! Are you okay? Lonzo told me to do it. Please don't be angry."

"She has been talking about you all night, Isobel."

I willed my racing heart to slow.

"How? Why?"

"Katy and I need to confess something. You know how obedient Katy is, never a minute's trouble. I just happened to see her holding her stomach after supper so I followed her to her room. I checked her myself before deciding it was only a stomach ache. I brought her to my room and told her we were going to play a little game. I then asked Dr. Helsley to come and check her for cholera, that she was deathly ill.

"She is quite the little actress, you know. I told her to wail and thrash with pain when Dr. Helsley came to check her. She even gave me a little scare. She almost had me convinced that she had cholera by the time he left. I knew he wouldn't come close to her."

"How could you do this, Lonzo? Why put me through such torment? I have just been through the worst time of my life thinking I had lost her forever. How could you be so cruel?"

"That was the point. I had to make it believable. It was crucial that Dr. Helsley not smell a rat. There could be no doubt of your pain. You also had to come to your senses, Isobel. You and Katy can't continue to stay here. It's drawing the life right out of you. I had to let you see how you would feel without Katy, and cholera was the only way to convince Dr. Helsley that she was really gone. Now it is time that I get you and Katy out of here before something truly awful does happen."

I still had trouble comprehending what was happening. "Katy, run along now and bring me a wet cloth," Lonzo directed her. She brought it back and he told her to place it on my forehead. I sat for a few minutes, and slowly my thoughts returned, though it was as if someone else's voice was forming words and sentences for me.

Lonzo was right. Had I not promised God that if Katy lived I would give her a better life?

"Oh, Lonzo, how can I ever thank you for what you have done for us? You have given Katy back to me. I agree with you. I cannot allow her to stay here. You have made me face the truth."

"Don't give me all the credit. It was Annie's idea. She thought it up after I told her that I was checking on Katy for a troubled belly. It was then Annie said, 'That little girl hasn't got anything keeping her here since her mother died, and Isobel has given her life to these women. Now it's time we give her life back to her. It will be our Christmas present to Isobel and Katy.'"

CHAPTER 48

I was still trying to understand the many details to what Lonzo and Annie had done. The reality of what awaited me began to sink in.

"How can I leave? This is all I know. How will I support myself, or Katy? Dr. Helsley will never allow us to leave."

"What is this 'us'? There is no us," Lonzo said. "Dr. Helsley thinks Katy is dead. Remember? I watched him sign the death certificate." Lonzo's words brought me to my senses once again. "I know you have a friend in New York. Annie has heard you talk about how much you miss her."

Lonzo continued, "I bought you and Katy tickets for the train to New York City. You do as I say and everything will be fine. I have worked for Dr. Helsley a long time and I know how to talk to him.

"Write Dr. Helsley a letter asking him to relieve you of your position. Tell him you can't bear to remain here without Katy. Tonight I will hide you and Katy in the wagon; and early tomorrow morning when I go to Mountain Springs for supplies, you'll ride with me," Lonzo said with excitement in his voice. "Annie will slip the note under Dr. Helsley's door in the middle of the night. He won't even be awake yet when we leave."

"Oh, Lonzo, he will know you helped me. You will get in trouble. I know Dr. Helsley's fury, and I do not want you or Annie to feel it. I do not want him to take it out on the women either," I cried.

"He won't do anything of the kind," Lonzo insisted. "He thinks Katy's dead and he knows how much you loved that little girl. Just write that you would go crazy here with her memory haunting you. I'll let him believe you packed a bag and must have just taken off walking in the middle of the night. I'll take care of everything. I'll wait a few days and then bring him a piece of your clothing and say I found it down by the river and he'll assume you either fell in or jumped off the cliff. That'll be the end of you and any idea of his trying to find you."

"What about Annie and the women? How can I leave them?"

"The women will miss you, but you have to think of that little girl first. You have to do this for her and for yourself. You need a life, too. Annie and I will be just fine," Lonzo said with a smile. "We might not be the same color, but love doesn't know color. Annie is all I need to be happy. We'll take care of each other, and don't you worry any about the women."

Lonzo stood a bit straighter and said, "Annie and I will make sure to take care of everything, maybe not as well as you, but we'll do our best. It's either those women or Katy. You choose."

"I shall never forget you, Lonzo, either of you. I can find no words strong enough to express my gratitude," I whispered, as I gave Lonzo a tender kiss on the cheek.

"Just go," Lonzo said. "Take care of yourself and our baby, and be happy."

"I will never be able to repay you or Annie for the sacrifices you have made. You have given my baby back to me. You have given my life back to me. I give you my word, Lonzo, I will make a good life for Katy and myself; and I will not break that pledge. I will never forget either of you."

PART THREE

NEW YORK, 1916

CHAPTER 49

When Katy was born into this world, a destiny had been set for her that threatened her identity with insanity. Somehow, through the wonders of the mind, she escaped that curse.

The childhood she treasured so and laughed at heartily was no more than a child's fantasy. She had changed the hard and cold to soft and warm. She found answers where there were none and explanations where nothing could be explained. She had convinced herself and everyone around her that the world truly was a good place and bad things did not happen. Her soul knew no boundaries; *reality* was merely a word.

An imagination is a wonderful thing to possess, unless you have been possessed by an imagination.

CHAPTER 50

Katy's erect posture and high cheek bones gave her a regal look; her expression was that of someone who had experienced more of life than sixteen years. Callie would have been proud of the fine young lady Katy had become. To think she was the same age as I was when I came to America.

Norna and Philip had not asked questions when Katy and I appeared on their doorstep almost ten years ago. We both shared the same shade of red hair, so no one had questioned that she was my daughter. If Norna and Philip knew that she was not, they kept it to themselves.

Since coming to New York, Katy's mind had closed the door to the past. She exhibited no remembrance of our time in Helsley House. We never spoke of it to Philip or Norna, not even to one another. It was as if we had simply and magically materialized one day on Philip and Norna's doorstep.

"Could you please excuse me, Uncle Philip? Mother?" asked Katy.

"Of course, dear," Philip and I answered simultaneously. We seemed to do that quite often.

Over the past ten years I had come to admire and trust Philip as much as I did Norna. He truly was Norna's brother, in sincerity as well as in looks.

Katy's life had become quite ordinary. She attended school and lived in a loving home. Norna's intended role as housekeeper and cook never came to be. She had fulfilled her dream of writing and had become a suffragette and rallied relentlessly. What time she was not attending rallies, she was writing. She and Philip shared the duties of the house equally.

I became the housekeeper and the cook and took pride in doing both jobs, thankful for all Annie had taught me in the kitchen. Katy and I were blessed with a full and comfortable life.

Cooking, cleaning, and taking care of the people I loved made me feel close to the women at Helsley House. I, unlike Katy, had not entirely dismissed my past. I wondered how Lonzo, Annie, and the women had gotten along these past years, and whether Dr. Helsley and his methods ever changed for the better. I hoped all had turned out well, but dared not write in fear of Dr. Helsley finding me and perhaps forcing unwanted reports of the past on our lives.

CHAPTER 51

Shortly after moving in with Philip and Norna, I was taking an afternoon stroll, when only two streets over from their brownstone I saw what was Miriam's son Paul's law office. A sign with the name "Paul Cohen: Office of Law" was hanging above a door. My mouth flew open with excitement. It could not be! I entered and there stood the man with cinnamon-colored hair. A few gray streaks peppered amongst the cinnamon, but I knew it was Paul. I could only stop and stare.

"Do you remember me, Mr. Cohen?" I finally asked. "I came over on a ship with your mother, Miriam."

"Of course! I knew you looked familiar. My mother will be delighted to see you. I cannot wait to tell her. We live not far from here." He chuckled. "You must have dinner with us."

"So your mother is doing well?"

"Yes. She now has three granddaughters." His pride showed in his eyes. "She will be so pleased to see you."

I was overjoyed to hear of Miriam's good fortune. I had often wondered about her and her family. And to think she lived this close to Norna.

"Here is our address. How does Saturday night sound?" He handed me the address. "We'll look forward to your visit. She has talked of you often over the years. Once she even questioned me about searching for you, and then she reconsidered, thinking that was not such a good idea. Be sure to bring anyone else in your family with you. We will prepare a feast and have a celebration!"

I could hardly wait to get home and tell Norna. Though Norna and Miriam only lived a few streets apart, neither had known the other was so near. I thought back to our time on the ship; I was sure that Miriam had never mentioned her last name to Norna, and if they had passed on the street, they surely never noticed one another or Norna would have told me. This would make for a great surprise.

Two nights later, Miriam, her son, daughter-in-law, three granddaughters, Philip, Norna, Katy, and I had a marvelous dinner. The stories and laughter filled the room. Miriam screamed so loudly when she answered the door, I thought my eardrums would burst.

The years had been good to Miriam, or maybe America had been good to her. She did not look much older than she had on the ship. I wondered if she colored her hair as some women did, but there was no more gray in her hair than in Paul's.

Before dinner, I pulled Miriam aside. "Please do not ask questions about my life since our time on the ship. I will come back and explain everything soon."

"Is everything all right?"

I nodded.

We enjoyed a night of reminiscing about our journey to America. What stories we told! Though the years had moved on, it felt as though Miriam, Norna, and I were still on that journey, searching for what the future held.

Though Miriam and Elizabeth, her daughter-in-law, did not voice their opinions as loudly as Norna, they, too, were suffragettes.

Norna spoke with such zeal. "The rallies have grown in numbers and in intensity and could last all night, every night, if it were not for the fact that too many women are still frightened to voice their feelings aloud. I however, will not be one of them."

Miriam began to laugh loudly. "I do not doubt that for a moment."

"Nor I," I said. "Norna has become a very strong spokeswoman for the suffrage movement; she, in her tailored jacket and stylish fedora, battles relentlessly for the cause."

"I will allow no man the opportunity to advance in this world in a way that a woman cannot," Norna proclaimed.

I had heard her repeat this time and time again at conventions. In the passing of the years, Norna had stood bravely and fought valiantly for what she believed. *Thank God for women like Norna*, I said to myself again.

Norna had spent the night in jail numerous times due to her quick wit and assertion that she and every other woman of the world had the right to be heard. She articulated her feelings in the highest courts. Though Philip did not like seeing Norna put herself in harm's way, he would not think of telling her to stop. It did not take him long to convince Paul to serve as Norna's lawyer. Paul was more than happy to do it. I smiled, thinking of how he would have his hands full defending her.

CHAPTER 52

All continued going well until two months after Katy's sixteenth birthday, when Katy began crying out in her sleep. She complained of being haunted by terrible images. As her nightmares strengthened in intensity, I feared that something was dreadfully wrong with her.

As my apprehension about Katy's nightmares worsened, I decided it was time to tell Philip and Norna the truth of where we came from. If I was going to help Katy, I would need their assistance. I believed the cause of her nightmares was the past, and I did not want the memories to move stealthily in and ruin the life Katy had been given.

I could not wait another day. After Katy excused herself for the night, and I was sure she was asleep, I asked Norna and Philip If I could talk to them. Unlike most nights, there were no rallies scheduled.

Though it took every bit of courage I possessed, I told Norna and Philip the truth of Katy's birth and our life together. I explained about working at an asylum and Katy's mother's death, and how we escaped. I did not divulge the awfulness of it all. I could not bring myself to tell them the name or location of Helsley House, fearing Philip would want to go back and have words with Dr. Helsley. I needed Dr. Helsley to continue to believe that Katy and I were dead. I wanted the past to be dead.

"I can barely face the two of you," I said through tears. "I am sorry that I did not tell you the truth upon our arrival. I was not trying to hide it from you as much as trying to dismiss that it happened." Tears blurred my eyes. "However, that does not forgive my behavior. I apologize to you both. I did not mean to take advantage of you, but that is exactly what I did."

"No apologies are needed," Norna said firmly as she looked at Philip. "No one was taken advantage of. You did what you had to, and we understand. None of this changes our love for you or Katy."

"We had come to the conclusion that your past was something you dared not speak of, and felt that in time you would share it with us if need be," Philip said softly. "Tomorrow is a new day, and we will decide together what must be done."

"Thank you," I whispered under my breath.

I climbed into bed but slept very little. I could not stop my mind. What if Katy were going mad? What if the past took her from me?

With the morning light, I rose early and did not know if I feared or yearned for what the day would bring. I entered the kitchen with apprehension. "Good morning, Philip."

"My dear, you look dreadful. Did you get any sleep?" Philip asked.

"I am afraid, very little. I could not stop worrying about Katy. I heard her cry out in the night again. I looked in on her and she was thrashing about as if she were fighting off an army."

"Isobel, I assure you that Katy is managing her life quite nicely. She has dealt with the past to the best of her ability; she is extremely bright, and her mind is, in fact, operating remarkably.

I want you to read about what I am sure Katy is suffering from. It is called repression. I feel her subconscious mind is waking in her sleep, trying to reveal something," Philip explained. "It's something I have studied extensively."

The thought of Katy's mind telling her stories about the past terrified me, but I trusted Philip's knowledge. He was a remarkable doctor and years ahead in his study of the mind. He had often returned home, motivated from lectures given by Dr. Sigmund Freud. Philip had an entire section of the library filled with articles and journals pertaining to the mind and how the brain functions.

I had read some of the articles. Each time I escaped into Philip's library, it took me back to the time I found myself hidden away in Dr. Helsley's office, reading everything I could find.

"So you agree that Katy should hear the truth of who she is?" I asked. "I never wanted her to know that I was not her real mother or where she spent the first six years of her life. I just cannot bear to let her continue to have such frightful nights. I fear after what you have said that she is reliving her days in the asylum through her dreams. Her sleep continues to grow worse. She cries out with such suffering. I have to free her from the past. Her sanity is more important to me than anything else."

"I agree, and do give Katy the credit she deserves. She *will* understand. I have no doubt in that. Right now Katy's mind seems to resemble nothing more than a photo album that has been thrown together with little interest in organization or sequence, filled with photographs of people and places from long ago, trying to convince her throughout the night that they exist, that they are real. Yet, with each morning light she counts them as no more than nightmares that would best be forgotten. Only instead of forgetting, Katy cannot stop remembering. Do you understand what I mean by that?" Philip asked.

"Yes. But I cannot help but blame myself."

I recalled a poem I had written just the night before.

Faces

The dreams have set their faces free
To haunt her through the night
The blankness in their eyes to see
And fill her soul with fright
So now she stays awake to flee
Into the morning light

"I pray that the truth will set her mind free and that she will forgive me for my deceptions." I sobbed.

"You will see. Katy will respond as Norna and I did. There is nothing to forgive. You did what you had to do to save both Katy and yourself. Her mind is extraordinary, and it is time she knew the truth.

"I'm sure it will be difficult for Katy to understand everything at first. I am confident, however, that she will come to understand and love you all the more." Philip wiped a tear from my face. "You could not be any more of a mother if you had given birth to her yourself. You must be prepared for the possibility that she will become confused, but you will see that she will value your reasons in the end."

"I hope so, Philip," I said, through sniffles.

"Now, let us change our topic of conversation for the moment. If we are conveying truths of the past here, then I would like to share something with you." Philip sat back. "Norna is out for the morning, attending a meeting, and I do not have to be at the hospital for another hour; so now is as good of a time as any. Norna gave me permission to share her story with you if it ever was deemed necessary. I think it may help you understand that many people have secrets. It is not a sin.

"I know Norna has made references to living with our aunt in England. What Norna never told you is the reason she went to Liverpool to live with Aunt Iris."

"Are you sure Norna will not mind you telling me this?"

"I'm sure. We have discussed it in depth. She is not ashamed of it, nor has she tried to hide it. I think much like you, it was just too painful to discuss."

Before Philip could continue, Katy came waltzing through the door, her hair pulled back by Callie's ribbon. She took such good care of that ribbon. It was as beautiful as the day she found it. What would she think when she found out that it was not mine to give, but belonged to her real mother, made by her real grandmother? The thought brought such sorrow to my heart. I felt alone once again at the idea of not being Katy's real mother.

"You both must read my latest poem," Katy said. "I think it one of my best. Aunt Norna thinks so, too."

My World

Living in this world of mine,
People aren't a threat.
Warm and cold are both the same,
And raindrops are not wet.

Emotions are not meant to be,
Feelings are to fear.
Fullness is but emptiness,
True life is never near.

"How beautiful," I said. "I believe you are right, I do think it is one of your best."

I hoped that Katy did not hear the worry in my voice. The poem was beautiful, but alarming, as well. Philip later agreed.

Katy had a brilliant talent for writing. As she grew older, I had encouraged her to continue to write poetry about her feelings. My poems had helped me survive some very difficult times. We often discussed how much writing helped us to understand our thoughts and emotions. Katy also kept a diary. She said it contained her most intimate thoughts. It was the one common thread between Katy, Norna, and me. Norna had taught me the importance of writing, and I had passed that on to Katy. We all believed in the power of pen and paper.

CHAPTER 53

The underlying nature of Katy's poems made me apprehensive. She expressed sadness and an unease that seemed to lie just beneath the surface in her seemingly beautiful words. The jovial Katy who kept us in stitches with her atrocious humor could not have written them. They came from someone much darker, someone who knew despair. I was now, more than ever, sure of what I must do.

Maybe there truly was someone else hidden within Katy. Since that first time when she swore the eyes in the mirror were not her own, I had shrugged it off as merely a game. Perhaps I was wrong.

Had I not done the same as a child, making up stories to pass the time and take away the pain and loneliness? A question I had asked more than once.

As Katy left the room, I grew eager to know what Philip wanted to tell me. I needed to know the secrets of Norna's past if they could help. Who would have imagined all the secrets held within these walls?

When Katy returned to her room, Philip continued. "You see, Norna and I were on vacation with our parents in Greece.

It had been such a grand week, for it was the first week after I graduated from secondary school, and I was enjoying spending it with my family. I had just turned eighteen and Norna was only a few days from turning fourteen. The incident took place the last week before we were to return home.

"There had been a commotion in the distance; and then as we were crossing the street, a runaway horse pulling a wagon turned the corner and plowed straight into us." Philip hesitated for a moment before continuing. "Our father was killed instantly; the horse had crushed his skull. My mother suffered internal injuries and died a few days later. I suffered a broken arm, and though Norna was physically unhurt, she suffered a terrible blow mentally.

"The sight of the blood and the sound of the screams traumatized Norna, haunting and tormenting her for years. She no longer spoke and barely ate. I was going to attend medical school in America and could not care for her. If it had not been for the goodness of our Aunt Iris, I think Norna might never have recovered." Philip's voice remained firm.

"It was months before Norna spoke again and years before she could sleep an entire night without waking up screaming for our parents. As you can see, Norna has lived through terrors and, by all accounts, she has grown stronger because of it. Aunt Iris encouraged Norna to keep a journal of all her thoughts. I think that journal was the very thing that saved Norna's life."

No wonder Norna thought that pen and paper held such power. Somehow, her aunt's wisdom had saved us all.

"The horrible things that Norna suffered did not make her cower at life, but instead, filled her with strength and courage. She gained the ability to handle situations that could crush another. Such is the case with Katy. I believe the past will only make her stronger," Philip reassured me.

"Oh, Philip, I hope you are right. I am so sorry for your and Norna's loss. It must have been terrible for the two of you, losing your parents right before your eyes. That is one of the very reasons I try so hard not to be judgmental. Even the most cruel and harsh people have lived a life unknown to others."

Katy was strong and smart, and she was not a judgmental person. She would understand what had happened to her, to both of us. I just wish I were as sure of it as Philip. I would tell her soon, but not just yet. I needed a little time to get my nerve up.

CHAPTER 54

"Isobel, are you home?" Norna shouted. "I have something amazing to tell you. Isobel, where are you?"

"Here, Norna, in the kitchen. I was just preparing a little something for breakfast. Would you like some?"

"I could not possibly eat right now. I am too excited for food! You will never guess who is coming Thursday night to the rally. Guess! Just try and guess," Norna insisted.

"I could never guess, just tell me. Who, for heaven's sake, has you so excited?"

Before Norna could answer, Katy spoke. "I will take a guess. Is it Nellie Bly? I know you have been trying forever to get her here."

"No, but that was quite a guess; and, yes, one day I will get her to one of my assemblies, but not this time. No, this time I have convinced Grace Verne Silver to honor us with her presence. It will be a rally to remember. She lectures on socialism and labor reform as well as women's rights. We need as many supporters and people on our side as we can get. She is coming all the way from Portland, Oregon. Clear across the country. She is someone with influence," boasted Norna.

"My dear, Norna, are you on yet another of your great rally missions?" Philip asked, smiling at Katy and me.

I was glad to see Norna in such high spirits. After what Philip had told me the night before, I now understood that there was a time in their life he did not think he would ever see his sister smile again, let alone so filled with happiness.

"Pardon me, dear brother, but I am not on another great rally mission. I am on *the* great rally mission, and would you please refrain from making snide remarks about my rallies? My great meetings of the minds are no less important than yours. We will change the way America thinks every bit as much as you and your psychoanalysis."

If there was one thing we knew about Norna, it was not to take her passion for her cause lightly. As much as Philip liked to make her think he felt her meetings were nothing but a group of silly women, he really felt as strongly as she did about the cruelties thrust upon women by ignorant, frightened men. I was glad to know that some men were not like my father or Dr. Helsley. Philip and Lonzo had taught me that not all men were vindictive and demeaning to women.

While accompanying Norna to a rally last month, I had heard Mrs. Vira Boarman Whitehouse, the president of the New York State Suffrage party, speak. Norna was correct in thinking women were gaining momentum in achieving the right to vote. Mrs. Whitehouse spoke with a vengeance. During her speech, I could not help but think once again of Annie, as Mrs. Whitehouse compared suffrage to freeing the black men from slavery.

Annie would have been a strong advocate for suffrage. How I longed for her and Lonzo! Lonzo would have also been useful at the rallies. He could have helped protect the suffragettes from the enraged men who occasionally bullied and threatened the women.

I turned and spoke to Norna. "I have never heard of Grace Verne Silver."

"She advocates for women and particularly the labor laws pertaining to them. Her daughter, known as Queen Silver, is a child, but no less an advocate for women. They are a magnificent pair."

"If she is half the woman you make her out to be, then I would not miss it for anything. I will be there," I said, with strongly felt enthusiasm.

"Of course you will be there. We need every woman we can muster," Norna said, as she began working on yet another flyer.

"What about me? May I come?" Katy begged. "I am getting older, and I am as tall as Mother. May I, please?"

I did not give Norna a chance to answer. "Dear, you know how I feel about your attending the rallies. I could not stand the thought of your getting hurt. Until they are less volatile, I must insist you stay home. I promise, there will come a time when you will be allowed to go, just not yet, not to this one." I could see how disappointed Katy was.

With her shoulders slumped, Katy turned and walked back toward her room. I wanted to run after her and tell her she could go, but I knew that would be unwise. As much as I wanted to make her happy, the gatherings were dangerous, and more and more women were being arrested. I had even heard of children being severely injured during raids on them.

I tried to hide the violence from Katy so she would not fear for Norna's safety or mine. I was only kidding myself. Katy read the paper daily. She never missed Norna's column; and she searched the paper extensively for any reference to Norna's name, just as I had done years before.

I was prepared to allow Katy to attend a rally now and then, but not this time. I knew the more famous the speaker, the more dangerous the rally.

Hopefully, Katy would understand.

CHAPTER 55

I accompanied Norna to many events and lobbied alongside of her. We challenged many of the most influential men in New York and on more than one occasion, we found some who felt that a woman should be considered their equal but refused to voice their thoughts. Fear of ridicule and shame brought on by the overwhelming number of men who thought otherwise silenced them.

I was reluctant at first to make much ado, fearing that Dr. Helsley would see my name in the paper and realize that I had tricked him. But as the years passed, my fears had lessened and my bravery grew. I believed Dr. Helsley had much more to worry about than a matron he thought dead.

The last ten years had brought many changes to our lives and in the lives of many Americans. A few states had already allowed women the right to vote, but New York was not one of those states. The Nineteenth Amendment to the Constitution had not been ratified, and Norna would not slow down and rest until that was accomplished.

"Isobel, are you ready?" Norna called. "You do remember what tonight is?"

"Of course, I remember. I was taking time to clear my thoughts. I just need to talk to Philip about his and Katy's evening plans first. I know how upset she is that she cannot accompany us to yet another rally. I want Philip to pay extra close attention to her tonight." I said this knowing quite well that Norna knew that *clearing my thoughts* meant I had been daydreaming again. It was a habit I had found exceedingly hard to break.

"You know, I think you are being overly protective of Katy," Norna said. "She is becoming quite the young woman and is more of an adult than you think. I think you should let her attend more of the rallies. She needs to be able to express herself without fearing what others will think. She reminds me so much of myself."

There was a lot of truth in Norna's words. Katy was a strong young woman and she could be a vital part of the movement. She had an uncanny ability to empathize. She not only understood the feelings of others, but felt their frustration and sorrow. She would listen to the stories that Norna brought home and begin expressing such heartfelt outrage at the women's predicaments.

I could not stop her from feeling the excitement of it all. But for now, she would have to be content printing the flyers and helping Norna with her newspaper column.

"Katy and I have had such wonderful talks about women's rights. She knows so much more than you realize," Norna asserted. "She would be such an asset to our cause."

"I believe that too." I knew I sounded defensive. "I am just not ready to risk her suffering from the brutality of it all this soon. What if the police were to pick her up with some of the other women and toss her in a jail cell? I would be inconsolable. I think all of that can wait."

"Well, if anyone could handle a jail cell, it would be Katy," Norna replied. "She can adapt to difficult situations better than anyone I have ever seen. She's more mature than most adults I know."

"Maybe so, but I think I will still wait a bit longer to cross that bridge." I said.

"You win!" Norna snapped. "You are the mother and by far the biggest prude."

"Thanks. I love you, too."

"Anyway, when have you known my brother not to pay close attention to Katy? He adores her." Norna chuckled.

"I know. I think they have a better relationship than Katy and I have," I admitted.

"Don't be silly. Katy absolutely worships you."

How I hoped that was true. I did not want anyone to replace me in Katy's eyes, not even her real mother.

CHAPTER 56

The time had come. I could not put it off any longer for fear I would never do it. Katy was suffering, and she had the right to know why. I asked Norna to join us but she felt it better if I spoke to Katy alone.

On a stifling hot afternoon one month to the day after I talked to Philip about my decision, I asked Katy to sit down and have a glass of lemonade with me.

"Katy, I need to speak with you. First, I want you to know how much I love you and how much I want to protect you," I said slowly. "I have never wanted anything for you other than love and happiness."

"There is no need to say such things. I have never for one second felt anything else," Katy insisted. "You have never ridiculed or chastised me, as I have seen other mothers do to their daughters. You have never made me feel anything but loved. What are you trying to tell me?"

I felt as if I were suffocating. Would Katy forgive me? Would she hate me? If only I could be as sure as Philip.

"Katy, what is your first memory?" I asked.

"What an odd question! I'm not sure of the answer. Does this have anything to do with the dreams?" Katy looked puzzled. "I know how much you have worried about my nightmares."

"They have been becoming worse, am I correct?"

"Yes. At times I can no longer distinguish between what is a real memory and what is a memory merely made of restless nights and unsettled dreams," Katy said, as thunder rumbled in the distance.

I hoped that was not some kind of omen.

"That is precisely why we are having this conversation. I have noticed how much the nightmares upset you. I can see it in your face and hear it in your cries at night. I have not been true to you, or fair. You need to know the truth." My voice quivered.

"Mother, you frighten me. Please tell me what it is."

"I know by reading your poems that darkness haunts you. Now again, I must ask again, what is your first memory?"

I thought of one of her poems that had made me shiver.

Childhood

Yesterdays we think are gone,
Although they're still around,
For as we make our every move,
Yesterdays are found.

We see them in the way we walk,
The way we laugh and cry.
They're found inside our every thought
Until the day we die.

Many say they're gone for good,
No one can bring them back.
But they're still there inside our minds
Ready to attack.

CHAPTER 57

I told Katy everything. Not once did she interrupt me or ask any questions. How could she sit so long and listen so carefully without so much as a change in her expression?

I did see her flinch, just a bit one time. How could she keep from lashing out? How could she not hate me for my deception? How could she not scream and cry out at the injustices that life had handed her?

I should have known it was not Katy's style to sob and whine. Katy had always been steadfast, which is exactly why she had survived. Still, I could not bear the silence.

"Are you finished?" she asked.

"Finished with what? The story?" I let out a long breath. "I have shared with you all I know. I pray to God for your forgiveness. I may not have done the right thing by you, but I did the only thing I knew to do. I could not bear to lose you or your love for me. Please forgive me and know that I love you more than anything in the whole world. Never would I intentionally hurt you or try to separate you from your real mother. I did everything in my power to get Callie to see you for the remarkable baby you were. I begged her to find no fault with herself and free herself to love you. She could not do so."

"How could you possibly think I would do anything but love you?" Katy said. "It is not such a shock as you would think. I knew that my life was not what it seemed to be. I never doubted your love for me, nor Philip and Norna's, but I knew a piece was missing."

Katy sighed. "As confusing as the dreams were, I could see a truth in them. I knew the women's faces were real. I knew the woman you call my real mother was connected to me in a strong way. I could hear her cries at night and see her hands reach out to me. But I must admit that I would not have dreamed my grandfather to be such a villainous person. How could he commit his own daughter to an insane asylum? How could he hate her that much?"

I could not bring myself to tell Katy the worst of it. I did not want any more lies between us, but for now, I could not tell her that her grandfather and her father were the same.

Katy smiled at me. "How could you think I would love you any less? Do you know how much better it feels to know that my dreams were, in fact, real memories? It is much better to have a crazed past than a crazed mind," She brushed her cheek with the back of my hand.

"How could I hate you when you gave me all I have? You gave me love, a home, Uncle Philip and Aunt Norna. You gave me my life and all else with absolute love. That you would believe that I would think differently is the only thing that really shocks me. You are my mother and always will be."

How could I have doubted Katy and her loyalty? How could I have doubted Philip? He knew how Katy would react. I was never as proud of anyone in my life as I was of Katy at that moment. I had only been happier once before and that was when I had found her alive.

CHAPTER 58

I t was a beautiful night. I had spent the afternoon with Miriam and given her the explanation I promised her. She, like Katy, was strong and forgiving. She only cried and comforted me, as she had done so long ago.

Upon returning home, Katy grabbed my hand and asked for my presence in the library.

"Is something wrong?" I asked.

"No, I would like to make a request. But first, I must ask Uncle Philip to join us, because this includes him."

Whatever was Katy thinking? Now worry set in. Philip and Katy returned shortly.

"Thank you both so much for coming," Katy said, most politely. "I would have had Aunt Norna here also, but I did not want to interrupt her meeting.

"Uncle Philip, I must ask a favor of you, for Mother will need your assistance if she is to honor my request." Katy sounded so mysterious.

"I want you both to know that I have given this much thought. I have never known a grandparent. Both of my mothers' parents and both of your and Norna's parents have passed on.

I would like to know what it feels like to have a grandparent. I want us to find Callie's mother, my grandmother."

"I disagree," I mumbled.

Katy pointed in my direction as she continued, "You are my mother, but Callie's mother is my grandmother. If she is still alive, I want to talk to her, I want to know her. I want her to know the truth. Could we please try and find her? I could never rest again if I thought we did not try. I owe Callie that much; we both do. She did bring me into the world. Uncle Philip, please convince Mother to do this. It is the right thing to do."

My mind was going in circles. I had not even imagined Katy wanting such a thing. I have to admit, that I, too, had often wondered about Katy's grandmother. I did not know if she knew about Callie's predicament or not, but I did not want Katy disappointed by this woman if she did know. Nor did I want Katy to know the truth about her father. How could I follow through with this plea? I found it odd that Katy did not even ask who her father was. I supposed she thought it did not really matter, or maybe she thought Callie never told me.

"Katy, what if Callie's mother did know where she was? What if she was not as loving as Callie made her out to be? Maybe Callie only remembered her the way she did because she could not live with knowing her mother deceived her, as well. There is so much we do not know."

"I did not have a grandmother before; and if Callie's mother, my grandmother, turns out to be indifferent or unkind, then I will tell her that Callie was too good a daughter for her, and I will again be without a grandmother. I have nothing to lose," Katy insisted.

"There is something I am afraid you did not think of. What about Callie's father? He left Callie in an insane asylum. I would put nothing past him, even murder. He might try to hide what he did and threaten us. You know he will deny his part in

Callie's fate. Can you accept that? He could be dangerous. Is he someone you would want to confront?"

"Yes, he is someone I also want to meet, for I will tell him, too, how Callie's life ended and what a pitiless human being he is." It was as if Norna were speaking through Katy. How alike their confidence was! Katy continued, "I am not afraid of him. That is where you come in, Uncle Philip. I not only want you there for guidance and counsel, but in case Callie's father becomes violent, you can bring your gun."

"Katy. When did I teach you to use such violence?" I asked, in shock.

"I did not say Uncle Philip had to use the gun, just show it; but if there ever were a need for violence, this is the time."

"I am afraid it is not all that easy," Philip said. "But it seems as if you have thought this out, Katy. Are you sure you want to pursue this?"

"I am quite sure. I knew there was more to my life. In telling me the truth, my mother brought my nightmares to life. Now I must act upon them to rid myself of them."

"I think your mind is made up, Katy. Do you agree to do this, Isobel?" Philip turned to face me.

I did not know if it was a wise thing to do or not, but I did feel that I owed it to both Katy and to Callie. I could not hide any more of Katy's life from her; I did not have the right. If she wanted to meet her grandparents, then she would meet them. In my heart, I knew Katy could handle the truth of her father's true identity. Katy was right. Callie did deserve justice.

"I do agree," I said. "Katy has convinced me it is the right thing to do. She would do well on a debate team. I do not, however, think it will be easy, but most things worthwhile are not easy. I am aware of the town where Callie lived, but I do not know if her parents are still living there, or if they are still alive."

"I can have Paul check into that," Philip said. "It will not be hard to find out. I will call Paul and have his law office begin immediately. Between Norna and Katy, this household will keep him in business." Philip laughed.

"What about your work? Will you be able to go with us?" I asked, knowing the answer. Philip would never allow anything to get in the way of Katy.

"The hospital can go on without me for a few days," Philip concurred. "I am not in the middle of anything that cannot wait. I will make arrangements and we will leave as soon as Paul concludes his investigation." Philip began jotting some notes on a piece of paper.

I did not think it so easy for Philip to miss work, but I knew he would not disappoint Katy. I believed he, too, was curious about her grandparents.

"When Aunt Norna returns home I will tell her of our plans."

Norna would be glad that we were going in search of Katy's grandparents.

My breathing became shallow as I imagined what we might find at the end of our journey.

CHAPTER 59

Paul quickly found the information we needed. Callie's parents had not moved, but Callie's father had died. He would never have to reveal what he did to his daughter. He would never hear how she had died, so alone and frightened. Katy would never get to confront him, but I was thankful Katy would never meet the man.

Philip sent a brief telegram to Callie's mother stating that we needed to speak with her, giving no indication exactly as to what, only that it was vital that she hear us out. He also included the date of our arrival.

So much had happened in a mere week's time. The train station was crowded but the train was on time. I was grateful for that, for I did not think my nerves could stand much waiting. We boarded the train and were on our way. This train was much like the one Dr. Helsley and I had taken from New York City so long ago. It seemed as though it were just yesterday I was traveling into the unknown, and now, twenty years later, I again found myself traveling in another situation that was just as uncertain.

Would we find a cruel woman or a broken mother? I had not even thought about brothers or sisters. Did Callie have any? None existed before she entered the asylum, but who knew what had happened after that. With each passing moment, I could feel my heart beating faster. I looked down and my knuckles where white from my clinched fists. My nerves were much worse than I had expected.

"Relax, Isobel," Philip whispered. "Katy is a strong young woman. Have you not learned that by now?" He sounded almost amused. "She can handle whatever comes her way. We all can handle it, as long as we are together.

"Do not think of the worst. Close your eyes and take a nap, and I will wake you when the noon meal is served."

I closed my eyes, and it was then I thought of Norna. She was extremely excited about a guest speaker she had asked to speak at her next rally. In all the excitement of our upcoming travels, I had forgotten to ask her who it was. I would have to remember to ask her as soon as we returned home.

I turned my head toward the window and began to feel a bit calmer as I watched the world go by. The mountains were beautiful. Once again, I remembered my train ride to Helsley House, the first time I had seen mountains in America. I had been so full of wonder and hope, eager to start a new life. So full of dreams for what awaited me. What awaited me had been far from hope.

At the time I believed I would be forever out of the grips of a pitiless and vile man. No such luck. I had been thrust into the care of another man with the same attitude toward life. I could not help smiling. I had shown both of them. Life at Helsley House may not have been easy, but it had been meaningful. I found friends, and even a daughter. I had loved and had been loved.

CHAPTER 60

As I peered out of the train window, I could hardly believe my emotions—I missed the asylum. Not really the asylum, but the women, and Lonzo, and Annie. I had grown in Helsley House. I had become a woman, a friend, a comforter, and even a mother.

My father had miscalculated my weaknesses. He had sent me there to wallow in despair, but I had not. I took pride in that thought. I wondered what happened to my father, if he still worked in the pub. Whatever the answer, it no longer involved me. He ceased to be my father when I arrived in America. Before that, he really had never been a father, anyway, only an overseer, who did very little overseeing.

Through the years, I knew I could have told Philip the name and location of the asylum. He could possibly have closed it down, but I dared not expose Katy to the past. Upon our return to New York, I would tell Philip about Helsley House. I no longer had anything to fear. Katy knew about the past and all it held. I prayed the women had survived Dr. Helsley's cruelties and that Lonzo and Annie were safe. I prayed they would have forgiven my selfishness. I may have acted cowardly in running from Helsley House, but I could not risk Katy's well-being.

"Wake up, Isobel," Philip said hurriedly as he gently shook my arm.

In all the excitement I had actually fallen asleep. As I turned and looked out the window I noticed the sun was already beginning to set. I could hardly believe I had been asleep for so long. It must have been the mental strain. Whatever it was, I was grateful for the chance to relax.

"You were sleeping so soundly I could not stand to wake you. You slept straight through the noon hour. We are being assembled for dinner."

The rocking of the train must have been like the rocking of a cradle. No wonder babies slept so soundly.

"It is quite all right, Philip; you were wise in doing so. I appreciated the sleep much more than I would have a meal. However, I am most definitely ready to eat."

We moved into the dining car. It seated thirty-two people. I knew this only by listening to the porter tell the people in front of us all about the train. The table was set with white linens, fresh cut flowers in urns, and wine glasses beside each plate. It was quite pleasing to the eye. The train rocked, but the waiter never spilled a drop. Philip and I both chose a red wine, while Katy asked for a glass of lemonade. Our meal was cooked and served as well as in any fine restaurant. We dined on cream of barley soup, roast duckling in mint sauce, creamed carrots, and boiled new potatoes and enjoyed a dark chocolate cake for dessert. Katy ate hers and half of Philip's, as well as some of mine.

After dinner, Katy was off and about sightseeing. She had taken up with a porter, who was only too happy to give her the details of the train. Her curiosity once again reminded me of myself on my first train trip in America.

"Where is Katy?" Philip asked.

"She is wandering through the train. She is so excited she can hardly sit still," I answered. "Philip, I hope Katy is not going to be disappointed. God only knows what we will find. It would be grand if Katy's grandmother turned out to be a kind woman and accepted her. It is going to be a shock for this woman. I have been so worried about Katy that I have given little consideration to the feelings of her grandmother. If she never knew what Callie's father did, we are going to bring great sadness into her life. I hope her heart can take it," I said with a sadness I had not thought to feel before.

"You are right to worry this time. How terrible to be told how your daughter's life ended! This is not going to be easy for anyone. But then again, I have questioned why Callie's mother was not there to protect Callie? But who was I to judge?" Philip asked, almost to himself.

Katy was excited at the thought of getting to sleep on a train. I hoped that I could still sleep after having already slept so much of the day away.

The train whistle blew and the conductor announced another stop.

CHAPTER 61

B y the time the porter announced our stop the wonders of the train had worn off and we were ready to be on solid ground.

The hotel was not impressive, but it was clean and comfortable. We washed our faces, changed our clothes, and went out to see the town.

Katy had brought a book with her on the state of Kentucky. Before reading more than a few pages, she informed me that it was not a state at all, but a Commonwealth. She wanted to know all about where her grandmother lived.

"Callie told me a few things about her hometown, Versailles. She told me it was in the area known as the Bluegrass Region. Some of the fastest racehorses in the United States were raised in this region. One of their horses had come in second at The Kentucky Derby in 1895." Boarding and racing horses were about the only things Callie ever mentioned about her family.

I smiled as I remembered Callie's love for her horse, Jameson. She wanted him to be one of the greatest racehorses of all times. She hoped that one day he would win The Kentucky Derby.

"Callie would sit and talk to Lonzo, Annie, and me all about the derby, how it was always held on the first Saturday in May. How it was held in Louisville, at Churchill Downs. She told us how the first derby had been run in 1875 and was won by a horse named, Aristides. Callie talked about all the money that was lost and won at each derby, more money than any of us could imagine.

"Callie had talked about how the riders of the horses were mostly Negro boys. They were called jockeys." How I missed that Callie. The one so full of life and a future. I wiped the tears from my face.

"Do you realize we have talked so much that we have noticed very few of the sights we came out to see?" laughed Katy, trying to lighten the moment.

"We will go back to the hotel for a good night's rest, and then promptly after breakfast, we will make it a point to look around and see what we can find." Philip chuckled as he hitched his arms in ours, escorting us back to the hotel.

We were all so weary that we slept late and missed breakfast. Missing breakfast seemed to be common in my travels. We would ride out to Callie's mother's ranch after our noon meal.

"What can I get you?" asked a large, imposing edifice of a woman. If her weight was any indication of the food, it was sure to be a fine meal. We examined the menu. There was quite a variety of food. There was nothing quite like good Southern cooking, or so I had heard many times from Annie.

"We have decided on the fried chicken, mashed potatoes, and green beans, please," Philip said, as he laid his napkin upon his lap.

Katy and I always had the habit of ordering the same meal that Philip chose. Katy was easy to please, and I always thought everyone else's food looked better than mine.

"Don't forget the banana pudding," Katy added quickly, before the large waitress left with our order.

"Oh yes, and we would like to order banana pudding for dessert, please," Philip added with a grin. "I am glad to see this ordeal has not hampered Katy's appetite."

Katy ignored his comment. "Do you think anyone here knows my grandmother?"

"I am not sure, but more than likely, they do. Be patient, Katy, later we will meet her and you will have your answers. Remember, this may not turn out how you have imagined," I said, as Philip shook his head in unison.

"I'm sure Callie's mother did not know the truth behind what happened," Katy said, wide eyed and assured. "I just feel it in my heart. She could have never been so cruel. I just can't believe that."

How I hoped this situation would be in Katy's favor. "I pray you are right, dear. I do not wish to think Callie was so fooled by her mother. One malicious parent is enough."

CHAPTER 62

After we ate we sent a telegraph to Norna, informing her of our safe arrival. We should have sent it sooner, but had become distracted by the uniqueness of our experience and hadn't immediately found a telegraph office.

I could hear Norna now: "How dare they not send word right away? Do they think I have nothing better to do than worry about them?" Norna loved to carry on. We all knew that it was just her way of showing she cared.

We went back to our rooms to get ready for something I was dreading far more than looking forward to. As hard as I tried, I could not share Katy's positive outlook on the situation. It was going to be a long afternoon and evening. Anxiety over what was to come crowded my thoughts. Katy and I washed our faces and left our room to meet Philip downstairs as we had arranged. I considered suggesting that we wait until the following morning to go to Callie's farm, but I knew the suspense would be too much for Katy and Mrs. Crider was expecting us. I could not put it off any longer.

The buggy ride was slow, but the magnificent countryside we passed held our attention. As we approached Callie's mother's horse farm, I could hardly believe what I was seeing. Here were fields of the most magnificent horses I had ever laid eyes on. I had seen horses before, but none that compared to these. Callie's pride had been well deserved, that much was for sure.

The house was large and painted a brilliant white, and the miles of whitewashed fences were just as clean and bright. Callie's family apparently had even more money than I suspected. To think of Callie's last days locked up in Helsley House alone and poor strengthened my resolve to right the injustice.

We turned down the long tree-lined lane that led to the house. What were we getting into? Fear began to overwhelm me, not for myself, but for Katy. Would her heart be broken by a family that had already broken her mother's heart? I did not let myself think of Callie as Katy's mother often, but I did at that moment.

"I think Katy and I should stay back while you introduce yourself to Callie's mother and explain why we're here," Philip said, with just the slightest hint of nervousness in his usually calm, self-assured voice. "I am sure the brevity of my telegram has topped Katy's grandmother's curiosity and brought about many questions of her own,"

"Perhaps you are right. I do not want Katy's existence to come as a shock until I have explained about her," I replied.

Katy did not say a word. I think she was finally understanding the many ways this visit could go terribly wrong.

CHAPTER 63

I knocked on the door. A woman who I assumed was Callie's mother answered. I could not help reflecting on what Callie's father had done, and a memory of a poem I had written several years ago flashed through my mind.

The Beast

Control the beast
That has no name
Its eyes are cold
They bear the shame

The beast shows force
For only one
When anger calls
It has to come

"Are you Mrs. Crider?" I asked.

"Yes, I am, and you must be Miss McFadden? We have been waiting your arrival."

From behind her I saw a deeply tanned woman, her face full of concern.

"And this is Manny, my dearest friend." Mrs. Crider said.

"Hello, Manny," I said as I smiled her way.

I had almost forgotten about Manny. I felt uncomfortable showing her less respect than I did Mrs. Crider, but Callie had never told me Manny's last name. Callie had told me little of her family, other than all about their horses, but she had mentioned Manny. Callie described Manny as a young Indian woman who Callie's grandfather had hired to help Callie's grandmother.

Mrs. Crider opened the door wider and allowed me to enter. "Now that we have all established who we are, would you please come in and have a seat. Since receiving a telegram from Mr. Philip Strom, I must say with each day's passing I have become more curious about why you feel such a need for us to talk.

"It is quite clear that you have information concerning my family that I need to know. I, however, cannot guess what that might be." Mrs. Crider said, as she directed me toward a seat next to the window. She and Manny sat together on the sofa.

I could tell by Manny's watchful expression that she was very protective of Mrs. Crider. Manny looked from Mrs. Crider to me and then back to Mrs. Crider again. As I tried to carefully choose my first words, I continued to see the concern in Manny's eyes.

At that moment I do not know who was more uneasy, them or me. I felt hot as the perspiration began to drench my skin, and I hoped the fear I was feeling did not show.

"I would like to get right to the point." I took a breath and swallowed hard. How was I ever going to say what needed saying?

"Miss McFadden, would you like something to drink before you begin?" Mrs. Crider asked.

"No, thank you. It is best if I just say what needs saying. It has been delayed long enough," I said. "Mrs. Crider, please excuse the questions that I am going to ask you, but I promise they are necessary. They are not intended to hurt or upset you." I was sure Mrs. Crider could hear the distress in my voice. "You will see their value when I am finished. Even though you do not know me, could you please trust me enough to answer my questions before you ask any of your own?"

"I … I will try, though I am not quite sure what to make of any of this." Mrs. Crider stumbled with her words as she tried to force a smile.

Manny spoke. "I don't know what game you're playing with Mrs. Crider, but I think you should explain yourself right now."

I could see she was growing more upset by the moment.

"Lynnette, you do not have to answer any of her questions if you don't want to. She will only upset you." Manny patted Mrs. Crider's delicate hand.

"I assure you, that it is not my intention. When I am finished you will understand why I am here, and why this is so hard." I took a breath.

"Continue, Miss McFadden. I will listen. Manny and I take care of one another. We have no family left, only each other." The love between the two women was evident. I thought of Norna and me.

"Thank you, Mrs. Crider. Now could you tell me when and where your daughter Callie died?" I asked.

"You knew Callie?" Mrs. Crider asked with surprise in her voice. "I'm sorry. I know you asked me not to question, but this is very difficult. How could you have known Callie? Of course, I can answer that. Callie was my only child." She lowered her eyes. "How I miss her."

Mrs. Crider continued. "It was sixteen years ago, April 6, 1900, that awful day when Beckham, Callie's father, came back to the house with Callie's sweater. It was muddy and wet.

Beckham said that Callie had taken off on Jameson, her horse. Callie had tried to cross the creek, but the water was up from a hard rain and she didn't make it. Although we never recovered her body, it was clear that she had drowned."

It reminded me of the story that Lonzo had invented to tell Dr. Helsley of my so-called death. Our lives were twisted in between lies and more lies.

Manny began to weep. "Lynnette never gave up. She went out day after day, night after night, calling Callie's name, begging for Callie to answer. Lynnette got so sick herself that we almost lost her. She caught pneumonia and was weak for months. It nearly killed her, and me. I loved that child."

What a relief! Callie's mother did not know. She was not a monster like her husband. I hoped Callie was looking down from heaven and hearing all this. *Callie, you were right to believe in your mother. She did love you,* I whispered in my heart.

As much as I despised what I was doing to these two gracious women, I could not help feeling jubilant for Callie. Callie's mother was a victim, just as much as Callie had been. Callie was right to put her faith and love in her mother. What a monster Callie's father was! I regretted the pain I was causing, but there was no way around it to reach what I hoped would be acceptance, or at the very least, relief.

"May I ask you a very personal question, Mrs. Crider? Were Callie and your husband close? I mean, was he a good father to her, or a good husband to you?" I knew this question was more personal than I had the right to ask. But the answer was one I needed.

"Miss McFadden, I am not sure what business that is of yours, but I will tell you, my husband was not a kind man, to Callie or to myself. He died three years ago, and I do not guess that it matters much either way. He was not only an unkind man, but, in fact, he was a bad man, a very bad man. I did not know that when I married him."

I understood why these women were so fearful of me and my questions. Who was I but a total stranger to them? Why should they believe anything I said? Maybe they suspected I was here to expose all their past secrets and shame? They had no idea who I was or what I was after. I could not expect them to tell me everything without something in return, yet I could not expose Katy, not just yet, not until I knew more.

"I will tell you some of what I know and I promise you it is the truth. I apologize again for the pain this brings to you." I took a deep breath and began sharing Callie's story.

"I think your husband was much worse than even you knew. I have met your daughter, and we became good friends."

"How could you have met my daughter?" asked Mrs. Crider, bewildered. "Before her death she and I were never separated. Not even for one night. I would have known if she had met you."

Manny stood up, tightening her grip on the edge of the sofa. "You are wrong. I do not know why you say such nonsense. You lie."

"I assure you, it is no lie." I prayed I would find the strength to continue. "I served as head matron of Helsley House Insane Asylum in West Virginia from 1896 until 1906. During those ten years, I saw things I would have much preferred not to."

I could see the alarm on both women's faces. The mere mention of an insane asylum was enough in itself. Both women must have been in shock, for neither uttered a single word. I carried on, with my hands tucked under my legs.

"A young girl by the name of Callie Lynn Crider was brought to us in April of 1900." I refused to use the word *committed*. It somehow seemed much too insensitive. I continued, "Callie wore a beautiful pink lace ribbon in her hair, which she said her mother had given her for her thirteenth birthday."

I felt I had to share a piece of information that assured them I had met Callie. I proceeded with what I knew to be the truth.

Their faces paled; even Manny's copper skin faded to an ashen shade of gray.

"Callie's father, Beckham Crider, had somehow convinced a doctor to declare Callie insane, and hired a man to bring her to Helsley House." I proceeded to relate to them all that Callie told me about how her father had bedded her in the barn. I explained how Callie thought her father had been drunk and had mistaken her for her mother.

I stopped for a moment to help control the shaking I felt inside and to check on the well-being of the women.

"Should I go on?" I asked anxiously.

Both women were wordless but able to nod their heads up and down. I hurried on in fear that the women would believe Callie to still be alive. False hope was the worst kind of hope.

"This will be even harder to hear, and I assure you once again if it were not for a worthy reason, I would not bring this misery upon either of you," I promised.

Not once did the women interrupt me, nor take their eyes from me. I knew they were searching my face for some hint of deceit. "Callie remained at Helsley House until 1906, at which time she succumbed to cholera and died." I did not tell them about the pregnancy or the baby. Not yet. As I ended my story I was sure they knew I was telling the truth. I could see it in their faces. Horror is a hideous thing to look upon.

It was then that the wailing began. It flooded the room. It was like the sound of wounded animals. Mrs. Crider and Manny were in perfect unison with their cries, and it tore at my heart.

Tears flowed like the waters that Mrs. Crider believed had killed Callie. It was heart-wrenching to watch. I sat helplessly listening and watching as they openly grieved.

Finally, Mrs. Crider calmed herself enough to speak. "If Beckham were not dead, I swear I would kill him right now with my own hands. What has he done? What in God's name have I done?"

"It was not your fault, Lynnette. Please. You know what a heartless man Mr. Beckham was, especially when he drank," Manny pleaded, turning to me as if to demand words to ease their grief.

The only thing I could do was to continue. They no longer feared what I had to say; for they believed I had revealed the worst. They wanted to hear everything I had to say now. Before I could continue, Mrs. Crider spoke for a second time.

"It was my sins and my lies that killed Callie, just as much as Beckham's. How can I ever live with myself? It was my lies that killed Callie. My dear baby girl died because of my sins. God forgive me. I might as well have killed her myself."

Once again, they both wept uncontrollably. Manny was patting Mrs. Crider's face, trying to console her as they both cried.

"Mrs. Crider, I do not understand your meaning. I only know that Callie did not believe that you were a part of Mr. Crider's plan to bring her to Helsley House. She loved you dearly, both of you."

Though I meant the words to comfort, they did not, and the wailing rose louder.

CHAPTER 64

Philip and Katy surely heard the heartache coming from inside the house. Katy was so anxious. I hoped they would not enter until I called for them.

Mrs. Crider abruptly dried her eyes and turned to face me.

"You must think me a fool. Well, you are right, I am. Now, it is my turn to tell you, what I know to be the truth.

"My father hired Manny to help my mother when he brought my mother to America. My father had met my mother in France. He had traveled overseas to look at horses he was hoping to purchase. My mother, Rosette, was frail and did not take well to living on a horse farm. One day, when my father went to Lexington, he came back with Manny. Manny had a young son, Joe, just two years old. Joe's father had been killed before he was born.

"Manny took care of my mother and never left her side. I was born a year after Manny arrived. My mother was not only a frail wife, but a frail mother, as well. Soon it was Manny who took care of both Joe and me."

Mrs. Crider hesitated for a moment. "Joe loved the horses and as he grew older he became a talented handler. He was good at breaking the horses. When Joe was old enough, my father hired him to break and train them. My father grew to love Manny's son as his own. Unfortunately, he never counted on Joe falling in love with me.

"I fell in love with Joe, as well." Mrs. Crider admitted. "I was proud of who he was. He was the most kind and gentle man I had ever known. His birth name was Dark Cloud. He had the blackest eyes I ever looked into.

"From the beginning, my father objected to our spending so much time together," Mrs. Crider said bitterly.

"Joe and I would slip off every chance we could get. We would ride the horses as hard and fast as the wind, over the hills and through the fields. We would lie under the moon at night and talk about the stars and the life we would someday share together," Mrs. Crider appeared lost in the past.

After another pause, she continued. "I had just turned eighteen when I discovered I was with child. I was afraid of what my father would do to Joe. The last night Joe and I were together, I told Joe about the baby. He wasn't afraid. He said he could convince my father to allow us to marry. The next day Joe was gone," Mrs. Crider said as she wept softly. "I never saw him again. I was heartbroken. I went in to town and asked everyone there if they had seen Joe, but no one had. My father said it was best for everyone. That Joe had a wild streak in him, but I knew that wasn't true. No matter how hard I tried to find Joe, no one would help.

"It also broke dear Manny's heart. She was the only one that defended Joe. She knew he hadn't just left, but she couldn't get anyone to listen to an Indian woman. My father and Beckham Crider convinced me that Joe had been talking in town about leaving. I was devastated. It was then I just sat down and gave up, and gave in to Beckham," Mrs. Crider said, while fighting back a new wave of tears.

"You see, Miss McFadden, Beckham Crider was not Callie's real father. Joe was. Callie never knew."

"Manny's son, Joe, was Callie's father? Manny is Callie's grandmother?" Would the secrets never end?

My mind was reeling. How could this be? The fears Callie had held on to so tightly were nothing more than lies. Katy had not been born to Callie's own father, but to a man Callie was not even related to. Thank God I had never revealed the truth as I had known it to Katy!

Poor Callie died thinking her own father was the father of her child. Mrs. Crider was right in thinking her lies and deceits had in fact partially killed Callie. Not intentionally, but nonetheless they had.

Mrs. Crider's words poured out. I sensed that she wanted to rid herself of all the long-concealed lies. "Beckham Crider owned the farm next to ours. That was my father's dream—that I would marry Beckham, join our land together, and make the largest farm in the county. I was so distraught when Joe left that when Beckham told me that Joe had had enough of ranching and taken off, I believed him. I should have seen through Beckham's lies, but I could not see past the idea that I, and my baby, had been abandoned. I should have known better.

"I married Beckham and let him raise the baby as his own." Mrs. Crider shuddered. "I felt if I could not have Joe, I did not care what happened to me or the baby. How selfish I was.

"After Callie was born, Beckham tried to love her, but every time he looked at Callie he saw Joe, and so did everyone else. He knew that no one believed her to be his own. Beckham with his fair skin, freckles and bright red hair, and Callie with her high cheek bones, olive skin and dark hair. She looked just like Joe." Mrs. Crider smiled as she peered out the window.

"The older Callie grew, the more she resembled Joe, and the more Beckham grew to hate her. He began to drink more and more and was harsh and callous with Callie and with me."

Mrs. Crider whispered something under her breath that I could not hear.

"I turned a blind eye toward it all. Manny tried to get me to see the truth, but I was too afraid to cross Beckham. I don't think I ever got over Joe's leaving. I never again felt the happiness or confidence I had with Joe." She looked at the floor.

"Near the end, Beckham stayed drunk, making rude comments and gestures. Whenever Callie questioned me about why her father hated her so, I lied and tried to persuade her to believe that he really loved her, that he was just overworked and sick." Mrs. Crider moaned. "I could not bring myself to tell her the truth. I could not tell her that her real father did not love her, either, and had abandoned her even before she was born.

"Manny threatened to tell Callie the truth and speak her piece to Beckham, but I refused to let her. Beckham would have killed Manny. I truly believed that, but I did not believe he was capable of killing a child. How foolish I was. It was only on Beckham's death bed that I learned the truth about Joe's disappearance.

"Beckham was dying from consumption when he started begging for me to forgive him for what he had done. When I asked him what he was talking about, that's when he told me what had really happened to Joe."

Mrs. Crider brushed her hand across her forehead, arched her back, and continued, "He followed Joe and me out into the woods that last night. He heard me tell Joe about the baby. He was enraged that an Indian had taken what he thought belonged to him. After I went home, he followed Joe and killed him. He buried him in the woods that night. I knew as time passed that Beckham had become capable of murder, but I did not know he had already done so.

"How could I have been so stupid? Joe never left the ranch. I should not have listened to all the lies." Her voice was hoarse with despair.

How sad that Callie would never know how much her real father loved her. I was struck by the bitter irony. Callie's whole world had been based on one lie after another. How I wish Callie could have known the truth. Yet, I would not have Katy if the past had been different. What a selfish thought right now.

It was true; the sins of our parents had been revisited upon us. I suddenly felt the need to protect Katy's grandmother. Though her lies had contributed to Callie's death, they were unintentional. Her husband had lied to her and deceived her, just as he had Callie. He had used her love and vulnerability against her. And I realized I had almost forgotten something very important. Manny was Katy's great-grandmother. Katy had two grandmothers.

I looked straight into Mrs. Crider's eyes and continued. "Mrs. Crider, you were deceived by a monster, just as Callie was. You were blinded by heartache; and although you were not there in the end for Callie, you must remember that Callie never doubted your love. She knew in her heart that you were not a part of Mr. Crider's plan to imprison her. You have to remember that. She loved you and Manny very much. Now, I must tell you both something I have kept from you." I spoke with a kind of authority I did not feel.

"Please, no more," Manny begged "Have we not suffered enough?"

"You have most definitely suffered, Manny. But you must look to the future now, not the past. You both can repay the love and devotion that Callie had for you."

"What future? How can we repay anything?" Mrs. Crider asked.

"Lynnette is right. We have no future. It has all been taken from us, my son Joe, Lynnette's daughter, my granddaughter, Callie. There is no future for us! Two old silly women, consumed by the past and all its lies." Manny cried in despair.

I could keep my secret no longer. "There is a future, a future you could never have dreamed of! The future that you, Mrs. Crider, and you, Manny, both have."

"What games are you playing, Miss McFadden? Are you here to mock our regret? What joy do you find in the pain of others?" Mrs. Crider's eyes held a sudden flash of anger.

I could have taken offense at her words, but I knew she only spoke them as remnants of the lies and truths I had brought to the surface.

"Mrs. Crider, Manny, you must listen. I have not told you everything. There is more."

The women looked at me with alarm.

"Say what you must. What more could there be?" It was not a question, but the words of a defeated woman.

I was reluctant to tell Katy's grandmothers that killing Joe was not the worst thing Mr. Crider had done. As the lies were torn down, the truth was built back, the whole truth. I had to tell them everything. I hoped it would make them stronger and not destroy them.

Philip and Katy must have been listening at the door, and before I could continue, they came bursting in.

Mrs. Crider and Manny looked at Katy, then looked at one another, then back again at Katy. Both women dropped to their knees and raised their hands over their heads.

"Heaven help us, Joe's black eyes and Callie's sweet face. Our babies have come home!" Mrs. Crider and Manny screamed.

The crying began again. Only this time it was a cry of resurrection.

CONCLUSION
1920

It was a terrible thing for Mrs. Crider and Manny to hear why Mr. Crider had sent Callie away to Helsley House. I was sure he did not know of her being with child. He just wanted the truth of his sins hidden away. Only by the grace of Katy's existence did they both escape facing the same pitiful and hopeless ending as Callie had had to endure.

Mrs. Crider's parents had both passed on a number of years earlier and she was the sole heiress of both her parents' and Mr. Crider's estates. She was a very rich woman and that money was now assuring that Callie's death was not in vain.

Mrs. Crider bought Helsley House, which was quite a chore, but with our friend Paul's knowledge of law and a few threats exposing Dr. Helsley for the man he really was, the purchase had gone through smoothly. Dr. Helsley's advanced age and poor health had taken the fight out of him.

Mrs. Crider replaced Dr. Helsley as owner and superintendent of Helsley House. Through many meals together, I had learned that Manny was a superb cook. She took up working in the kitchen alongside Annie. They were quite a pair.

Lonzo remained in charge of the gardens and maintenance. I cannot tell you how happy I was to reunite with Lonzo and Annie. What a joyous day that was.

Philip took over as the medical doctor. Though it took some time, he found a newly graduated physician to take over for him in New York, and he left his medical practice there. I became Philip's assistant and later his wife. Philip's knowledge of the mind came to great use with the women. They no longer suffered at the hands of cruelty.

It was as if none of us had ever been separated.

Norna remained in New York where she could continue to attend her rallies. She would be a strong advocate for the women of Helsley House.

On August 18, the Nineteenth Amendment to the Constitution was ratified, and on August 26 became law, securing for female citizens of the United States the right to vote. Still, women had a long way to go.

In visiting Helsley House Norna came across a class of women she had never encountered before: "the mountain women." Norna had found more women and more causes to fight for. She would not be satisfied until every single woman that lived was treated with no less respect than the man standing beside her. Norna now turned to concentrating her fight on equal pay for equal jobs for women. "It's just a matter of time," she said firmly, over and over again.

On returning home from our trip to Kentucky that first time, I remembered to ask Norna who the speaker had been that had excited her so. It had been none other than the great Nellie Bly.

Fate was like nothing else, for sure. Norna had explained to me that Nellie Bly was not only a strong advocate for women's rights but a great journalist, and that she had something in common with the women at Helsley House. While Nellie Bly was writing for *The New York World,* she had taken an undercover assignment where she pretended to be deranged, and after being examined by a number of influential doctors, she was committed to the Women's Lunatic Asylum on Blackwell's Island. The exposé she wrote afterwards proved that doctors knew very little about insanity.

Katy remembered everything of her past after returning to Helsley House. The past held no more secrets. Nights held no more prisoners. She continued to write and read her poetry to the women when she visited. She remained living in New York with Norna, where she enrolled in college to be a psychiatrist, following in her Uncle Philip's footsteps.

Helsley House Insane Asylum had a name change. It became known as Callie's Sanitarium, a place for the mind, soul, and body to be soothed and calmed. Holistic practices such as nutrition and exercise were proving to be of great benefit to the women.

"Dress loose, take a great deal of exercise, be particular about your diet, and sleep sound enough, the body has a great effect on the mind," Elizabeth Cady Stanton had said, and we found it to be true.

Kind words and comfort replaced brutality. For women who suffered extreme mental distresses, we remodeled a ward where they could be treated with Philip's knowledge of psychoanalysis.

Every woman has a purpose. We are all a family, closer than any blood family could be. We are confident and intelligent, and we are all stronger for what we have endured. We will no longer feel guilt and shame. We have survived and become stronger because of it. *May no woman ever again feel less than she is, for merely being who she is.*

AFTERWORD

As the 1800s came to an end, so did the Victorian era for women. As the 1900s emerged, the women's movement flourished, suffragists rallied, and society was never quite the same. The numbers of independent career women reached a new high. Women had found their voice.

My favorite book is *Jane Eyre*. I tend to be drawn toward books and films about young women being tossed aside by society and made to withstand horrible conditions. Jane was never actually committed to an insane asylum; however, she was committed to an institution for girls that was as badly run as many asylums were. The girls were there for the most part because they were just that, girls. Secondly, they were from poorer families, thrown away because they held no value to their families.

The history of mental institutions has intrigued many. From early days of being referred to as lunatic asylums, insane asylums, alms houses (which were actually homes for paupers but every bit as terrible), sanatoriums, mental institutions, mental hospitals, and the present day psychiatric facilities, asylums have been represented as dark and forbidden places, condemning those who have been committed to atrocities like none other. Society has hidden those people away and dictates that people do not discuss them, especially in front of children.

As the 1900s emerged and marched onward, asylums were most often full beyond their capacities. Though this book focuses only on women, many men were also committed. The facts have shown, however, that women suffered abuse by the system far more frequently.

Women were committed for many reasons, but very few had to do with genuine insanity. Women with hormonal imbalances and women under undue stress were once thought of as having neurotic tendencies, melancholy, and hysteria. Women were committed to asylums for having a voice, for being their own person, for owning something someone else wanted. A woman could be put away for years, if not forever, in conditions that were detestable, by only a single signature.

Not all asylums were like this; there were asylums managed by reputable people for a legitimate cause. Some people who were truly stricken with mental illnesses found help in such places to overcome their battles; this most often, however, was not the case.

The history of insane asylums has shaped our current mental facilities, as well as our modern day society. Psychoanalysis and journaling have been strong components of modern day treatment for coping, understanding, and overcoming the pain and stigma attached to mental illnesses.

The power of the pen and paper will prevail.

> I think, with never-ending gratitude, that the young women of today do not and can never know at what price their right to free speech and to speak at all in public has been earned. (Lucy Stone, one of the founders of the American Equal Rights Association)

APPENDIX

List of Poems